HENRY JAMES

The Turn of the Screw

古堡驚魂

Adaptation and activities by Janet Borsbey
and Ruth Swan
Illustrated by Rodolfo Brocchini

U0108895

The Commercial Press

Contents 目錄

故事錄音開始和結束的標記
start ▶ stop ■

The Governess

Miles

Flora

Miss Jessel

Peter Quint

Mrs Grose

Vocabulary

1a *The Turn of the Screw* **is set in a Victorian country house. Such houses had a very large staff. Match the household job in Box A to the job description in Box B. Use your dictionary to help you.**

A	B
governess gardener housekeeper butler housemaid lady's maid valet groom cook	a) was responsible for running the house b) made the meals for the family and the servants c) looked after the master and his clothes d) looked after the mistress and her clothes e) looked after the horses and stables f) was in charge of the other servants g) looked after and taught the children h) was responsible for the parks and grounds i) did the cleaning and helped in the kitchen

1b **Work in pairs. Discuss these points.**

- Which of these jobs would you most like to do? Why?
- Which would you least like to do? Why?

2a **Read this short summary of the plot of *The Turn of the Screw*. Tick the words you expect to read in the text.**

A nervous young governess comes to Bly to take care of two orphans. She finds herself in charge of them and the staff of a large country house. She begins to hear and see strange things and she is drawn into a battle to try and save the children. The consequences of her actions lead to a terrible conclusion.

☐ ghost ☐ death ☐ terror ☐ love ☐ murder
☐ fight ☐ possessed ☐ cruel ☐ sick ☐ disappear

2b Use your dictionary. Complete the word-building table.

noun	verb	adjective(s)
death		deathly/dead
	possess	
	disappear	*not applicable*
	not applicable	cruel
murder		
	love	
	not applicable	sick

3 Anagrams. Solve these anagrams to find the ten verbs we use to report speech. Then put them into the context phrases in the Past Simple.

1 mxcliea   'Oh no!' _____ Miles.

2 ryc   'Help!' _____ Flora.

3 kas   'Why are you here?' she _____ .

4 rwpheis   'Shh!' he _____.

5 pelry   'I don't know,' _____ the governess.

6 eaddmn   'Tell me now,' she _____.

7 ecionnut   'And another thing,' he _____.

8 aenrsw   'At ten,' they _____.

9 emrcsa   'There!' Flora _____.

10 ueinqre   'When?' he _____.

Speaking

4 Answer the questions then work in pairs to discuss your answers.

- What sort of books do you enjoy reading?
- Have you ever seen a horror film? Was it good?
- Have you ever felt afraid? Why? When?

Prologue

"Two turns of the screw."

2 It was Christmas Eve and there we were, listening to the story, sitting around the fire, holding our breath and, except for one or two comments about the scariness[1] of the tale, generally very quiet. Everything was as it should be; the story was strange, the house was old. Someone said that this was the only story he remembered where a child had been involved. It was the tale of an apparition which had taken place in a house very like the one where we were staying. A small child, asleep in his room, had been woken up by the appearance of this terrible apparition[2]. The child's terrified screams had woken the mother and, as she went to calm her child, she had seen the exact same thing.

The observation that it was unusual for such stories to involve children seemed to interest Douglas and I thought he might have a story he wanted to share, so I waited. Just before we all went to bed, he explained what was on his mind. 'I quite agree that Griffin's story of the ghost, or whatever the apparition was, was much more interesting because it first appeared to the little boy. I know of another similar story involving a child. If the child gives the effect another turn of the screw[3], what do you think about a story involving *two* children?'

1. **scariness:** 恐懼
2. **apparition:** 幽靈、幻影

3. **turn of the screw:** 擰緊鏍絲，比喻事情或氣氛越來越緊張

8

'We say, of course,' somebody exclaimed, 'that they give two turns of the screw! And that we want to hear about them.'

I can see Douglas standing in front of the fire, looking at us with his hands in his pockets. 'Nobody except me, until this moment, has ever heard this story. It is absolutely horrible.'

Several people, naturally, thought this made the prospect even more exciting, and our friend, with great skill, looked at each of us in turn and said: 'It's worse than anything. Nothing at all touches it.'

'For terror?' I remember asking.

'For dreadful[1] – dreadfulness!'

'Oh, how delicious!' cried one of the women.

He took no notice of her. 'For general ugliness and horror and pain.'

'Well then,' I said, 'just sit right down and begin.'

He turned to look at the fire and watched it for a moment. Then he turned to us again: 'I can't begin. I shall have to send to town for it.'

Everyone groaned[2] in disappointment, so he explained. 'The story's written. It's in a locked drawer. I could send the key to my servant and ask him to send the envelope to me here.'

It seemed as if he wanted us to encourage him, to stop him from hesitating. He had broken the ice, ice which had formed over many winters. The others were irritated that they couldn't hear the story immediately, but I asked him to write first thing the next morning, so that we could hear it as soon as possible; then I asked whether the story had happened to him.

'Oh, thank God, no!' he answered quickly.

'And were you the person who wrote the story down?'

'No, I have the impression *here*,' he put his hand on his heart, 'I've never lost it.'

---

1. **dreadful:** 可怕的

2. **groaned:** 抱怨

'Then your manuscript –?'

'Is in old, faded ink, and in the most beautiful handwriting.' He paused. 'A woman's. She has been dead for twenty years. She sent me the story before she died.'

They were all listening now, and some people, of course, were wondering about Douglas and the woman. He wasn't annoyed. 'She was a charming person, ten years older than I. My sister's governess[1],' he quietly said. 'She was the nicest governess I have ever known. It was a long time ago, and this story happened many years before that. I was at university, and when I came home the second summer, she was already looking after my sister. It was a beautiful summer and we often went for walks in the garden. We talked a lot and I thought she was extremely clever and nice. Oh yes, don't smile like that: I liked her very much and she liked me too. If she hadn't liked me, she wouldn't have told me the story. She had never told anyone.'

'Because it was so frightening?'

He continued to stare at me. 'You'll easily see why. You *will*.'

I stared back at him. 'I see. She was in love.'

He laughed for the first time. 'You *are* perceptive[2]. Yes, she was in love. I mean, she had been in love. That was clear. I remember the time and the place – the beautiful garden, the shade of the trees and the long, hot summer afternoon. It wasn't the place for a horror story; but oh –!'

He walked away from the fire and sat down in his chair.

'You'll receive the envelope Thursday morning then,' I said.

'Probably not until the second post.'

'Well then; after dinner–'

'You'll all meet me here?' He looked at us all again. 'Isn't anybody going?' He seemed to hope.

---

1. **governess:** 家庭教師   2. **perceptive:** 洞察力強

'Everybody will stay!'

'*I* will – and *I* will,' cried the ladies, although, earlier, they had been planning to leave.

Mrs Griffin wanted more details. 'Who was she in love with?'

'The story will tell,' I replied.

'Oh, I can't wait for the story!'

'The story *won't* tell,' said Douglas; 'not in any obvious way.'

'That's a pity. That's the only way I ever understand.'

'Won't *you* tell, Douglas?' somebody else asked.

He jumped up. 'Yes, tomorrow. Now I must go to bed. Good night.' And, quickly picking up a candle, he left us.

Mrs Griffin spoke. 'Well, if I don't know who she was in love with, I know who *he* was in love with.'

'She was ten years older,' said her husband.

'All the more reason, at that age!'

'And now he finally wants to tell the story.'

'This,' I replied, 'will make Thursday night interesting.' Everyone agreed with me and we could think of nothing else, so we all said goodnight and took our candles up to bed.

The next day, we discovered that a letter had been sent to his London apartment by the first post. We said nothing to him till after dinner, till the time of the evening that was best for stories containing an element of fear. Then he began to talk, just as we had hoped. He thought it was important to explain some things, on this second night, before the envelope arrived.

To cut a long story short, I should say that the manuscript arrived on the third day and that Douglas finally started reading it to the party on the fourth night. By then, some of the ladies had left the party. Their departure made our group more compact and select, and this only added to the atmosphere.

Douglas gave us this information in the form of a prologue. His old friend, the woman who wrote the story, was the youngest daughter of a country clergyman[1]. Her father was poor, so, at the age of twenty, she answered an advertisement to work as a governess. She was invited to London to meet her possible future employer. She arrived at Harley Street, a fashionable London address, and met the gentleman. He was impressive, unmarried and in the prime of life, a fine gentleman of the type she had only met before in her dreams or in old novels. This anxious, shy girl from a country vicarage saw a handsome, bold, pleasant man who was relaxed, cheerful and kind. She was impressed with his wealth, his good looks and his charm with women. His London residence was fine, full of souvenirs from his travels, but he wanted her to go to his family's country home.

The gentleman explained the situation. He was guardian[2] to his nephew and niece, because their parents were dead. The children were a worry for him, because they were young and because he was single with no children of his own. He was, of course, determined to do his best for the poor children, although he had made some mistakes in the past. The children lived at Bly, the house in the country, and he visited them from time to time, but it was very unfortunate that they had almost no other relatives and he was a very busy man. A servant, called Mrs Grose, was in charge of the house for the moment, and she was a very good woman. There were plenty of other servants to help, but the new governess would be in charge[3]. In the holidays, the governess would also have to look after the young boy. He was away at school during term time[4], despite being very young, but there

1. clergymen: 神職人員
2. guardian: 監護人
3. in charge: 看管
4. term time: 學期

really was no other choice. The children had had a governess before, but they had, unfortunately, lost her. It was a shame[1], she had been a respectable person and she had been the perfect governess until she died. Since then, little Miles had gone to school and Mrs Grose had looked after little Flora; there were also a cook, a couple of maids[2], an old pony[3], an old groom[4] and an old gardener, who were all very respectable indeed.

Douglas had told his story up to this point, when someone asked a question. 'And what did the former governess die of?'

Our friend answered quickly. 'That will become clear. I'm not going to tell you anything in advance.'

'But you *are* telling us things in advance.'

'If I were the new governess, I would want to know –'

'If there was any danger?' Douglas finished my sentence. 'She did want to know, and she did find out. You'll hear tomorrow what she found out. Meanwhile, of course, she was a little concerned at the responsibility. She was young, inexperienced and nervous: the position of governess seemed serious and quite lonely. She went home for a few days to consider the offer. The salary was very good and she soon returned to London to accept the position.'

Douglas paused and I decided to comment. 'The splendid young man! He charmed her.'

He got up and went to the fire and, as he had done the night before, watched it for a moment. 'She only saw him twice.'

'Yes, but that's the beauty of her passion.'

I was surprised when Douglas turned to me. 'It *was* the beauty of it. There had been other applicants for the position,' he continued, 'but they hadn't been charmed. The gentleman explained honestly

---

1. it was a shame: 可惜
2. maids: 女傭

3. pony: 小型馬匹
4. groom: 馬伕

that some had thought the position sounded boring or strange, or that they hadn't liked his main condition.'

'Which was –?'

'That she should never bother[1] him – but never, never: she should never write to ask him anything or to complain about anything. She had to solve all problems herself, be in total charge of everything and leave him in peace. She promised to do this and he was delighted. When he took her hand and thanked her for the sacrifice she was making, she felt rewarded[2].'

'But was this her only reward?' one of the ladies asked.

'She never saw him again.'

'Oh!' said the lady.

Douglas left and there was no more discussion of the story until the following evening, when, sitting by the fire, in his best chair, he opened the faded[3] red cover of a thin, old-fashioned, gilt-edged[4] album. The whole thing took more than one night, but, on the first night, the same lady asked another question. 'What's the title of the story?'

'There isn't one.'

'*I* have one!' I said.

But Douglas took no notice and began to read in a fine, clear voice which echoed the beauty of his author's hand.

---

1. **bother:** 打擾
2. **rewarded:** 得到回報
3. **faded:** 褪色的
4. **gilt-edged:** 鑲金邊的

FCE - Reading Comprehension

1 **Choose the best answer – A, B, C or D**

1 When does the story start?
A ☐ Christmas Eve
B ☐ Christmas Day
C ☐ New Year's Eve
D ☐ New Year's Day

2 What are the guests at the old house doing?
A ☐ telling ghost stories
B ☐ telling funny stories
C ☐ telling jokes
D ☐ telling lies

3 Why is Douglas's story unusual?
A ☐ it involves a child
B ☐ it involves two children
C ☐ it's set in an old country house
D ☐ it's a ghost story

4 Why can't Douglas tell the story immediately?
A ☐ the manuscript is in London
B ☐ he has to go to London the next morning
C ☐ he can't remember the ending
D ☐ he hasn't got the key to the drawer

5 How do people feel when they can't hear the story immediately?
A ☐ angry
B ☐ pleased
C ☐ disappointed
D ☐ tired

6 What does Mrs Griffin think?
A ☐ that it was a true story
B ☐ that the governess was in love with Douglas
C ☐ that Douglas was older than the governess
D ☐ that Douglas was in love with the governess

Reading Comprehension

2 Are these statements true or false? Correct the false answers.

		T	F
1	The governess is the daughter of a clergyman.	☐	☐
2	The governess's family is quite wealthy.	☐	☐
3	Her future employer lives in Harley Street.	☐	☐
4	The two children are called Miles and Flora.	☐	☐
5	The children's parents live abroad.	☐	☐
6	The children live in a country house called Bly.	☐	☐
7	Her employer wants to know every detail about the children's progress.	☐	☐
8	The governess never saw the children's uncle again.	☐	☐

Vocabulary

3a Divide the adjectives in the table into two columns. Which describe the governess? Which describe the children's uncle? Some adjectives describe both of them.

shy • fashionable • nice • clever • beautiful • unmarried • pleasant
young • handsome • charming • anxious • fine • impressive • bold

the governess	the children's uncle

3b Write a short description of either the governess or the children's uncle.

Word-building

4a Complete the table using words from the Prologue.

noun	adjective
dreadfulness	
	scary
	ugly
	beautiful
shyness	
respectability	
	disappointed
	painful

4b Complete these quotations from the Prologue with words from the box.

1 "Nothing at all that I know touches it [...] for _____ – dreadfulness! [...] For general _____ and horror and pain."

2 "Yes, but that's the _____ of her passion."

3 "Everyone groaned in _____, so he explained."

4 "There were also a cook, a couple of maids, an old pony, an old groom and an old gardener, who were all very _____ indeed."

Speaking

5 Work in pairs. Discuss the following points.

- Do you think being a governess would be a difficult job? Why/Why not?
- What do think the house at Bly will be like?
- Are you enjoying *The Turn of the Screw* so far? Why/Why not?

6 Read the letter below from Douglas to his servant and think of the word which best fits each gap. Use only <u>one</u> word in each gap.

Hudson,

I'm sure (1) _____ everything is going very (2) _____ at the house in London, (3) _____ usual.

I need you to do a couple of things for me.

First of all, I need a document from my study. You will find the document (4) _____ the top drawer of my desk. The drawer is locked, (5) _____ I have enclosed the key. Make sure that you lock the drawer again, then send the document and the key back to me, (6) _____ this address. Please wrap the parcel well, (7) _____ the document is quite old and is important to me.

Secondly, please forward (8) _____ messages for me in the same parcel.

Many thanks

PRE-READING ACTIVITIES

Listening

7 a What do you think? Are these statements from Chapter One true or false?

		T	F
1	The governess travelled to Bly by train.	☐	☐
2	The journey was very comfortable.	☐	☐
3	The governess expected the house at Bly to be light and happy.	☐	☐
4	Bly was a very fine house.	☐	☐
5	The little girl was a charming child.	☐	☐
6	The governess's room was large and beautiful.	☐	☐
7	Mrs Grose was a very elegant woman.	☐	☐

▶ 3 **7 b** Listen to the first part of Chapter One and check.

Chapter One

"Strangely at the helm."

3 I remember the beginning as a series of ups and downs.

After I had accepted the position and agreed to his condition, I had two or three very bad days. I was full of doubts, sure I had made a terrible mistake. I was in this state of mind as I sat in the uncomfortable coach[1] which was taking me to my new home.

At the inn[2], a small carriage[3] from the house was waiting for me and the drive through the friendly countryside, full of summer sweetness, seemed to change my mood. I began to feel welcome and my courage returned as we arrived at the house.

I had expected something dark and melancholy, but a happy surprise was waiting for me. I remember the pleasant impression of the front of the house, its open windows and the two maids looking out; I remember the garden and the sound of my wheels on the gravel[4], the tree-tops and the rooks[5] in the golden sky. The house and gardens were finer than my own poor home, and a woman and a small girl immediately appeared at the door. The woman curtseyed[6] to me as if I were the mistress of the house or a very important visitor. I felt I was going to enjoy my position more than I had expected.

My first impression of the little girl made me happy: she was such

---

1. **coach:** 舊時的公共馬車
2. **inn:** 小旅館
3. **carriage:** 馬車
4. **gravel:** 砌成花園小路的石子
5. **rooks:** 禿鼻鴉
6. **curtseyed:** 行屈膝禮

a wonderful child that I was very lucky to be able to teach her. I didn't sleep much that night, I was much too excited about everything. The large impressive room, the enormous bed, the fine curtains, the long glasses[1] in which, for the first time in my life, I could see myself from head to foot, were – like the charm of my small pupil – unexpected extra reasons for being happy with my position.

Another reason to be happy was the way I got on well with Mrs Grose. I had been rather worried about this relationship, but she had clearly been glad[2] to see me, almost to the point of not wanting to show it. She was a stout[3], simple, plain, clean woman. Why didn't she want to show she was glad? If I had been suspicious, I might have felt a little uneasy[4]. But was she honestly glad I was there? I could not be at all uneasy about my relationship with my beautiful angelic little girl, I was so looking forward to getting to know her.

I got up before morning and wandered[5] around my room. I watched the summer dawn from my open window and I listened to the birds as they started their morning song. There were other sounds I heard, or thought I heard, inside, not outside. I thought I heard a child cry in the distance; I thought I heard the sound of a light footstep[6] outside my room. It must have been my imagination. Or was it? Subsequent events made me wonder.

Looking after little Flora, teaching her and 'forming' her would make my life happy. From tomorrow, Flora would sleep in my room and her small white bed was already made. Last night, she had stayed with Mrs Grose, because I was still a stranger and she was naturally quite shy. I was certain that she would soon begin to like me and that this sweet honest child and I would become great friends. Mrs Grose was happy that I admired Flora. I could see that as we watched the

---

1. **glasses:** 鏡子
2. **glad:** 快樂
3. **stout:** 略胖的
4. **uneasy:** 不自在
5. **wandered:** 漫遊
6. **footstep:** 腳步聲

child eat her bread and drink her milk, although we couldn't say very much in front of her.

'And the little boy. Is he like her? Is he very remarkable[1] too?'

It was important not to flatter[2] children.

'Oh Miss, very remarkable. If you like this one!' – and she stood there with a plate in her hand, smiling at the little girl, who looked from her to me and back again, with calm, heavenly eyes.

'Yes, I do.'

'Then you'll be carried away[3] with the little gentleman!'

'Well. That's what I came for. To be carried away. I was carried away in London!'

I can still see Mrs Grose's face as she understood me. 'In Harley Street?'

'In Harley Street.'

'Well, Miss, you're not the first, and you won't be the last.'

'Oh, I know I'm not the only one,' I laughed. 'Anyway, my other pupil is arriving tomorrow, I believe.'

'Not tomorrow, Miss, Friday. He arrives by coach, as you did, and the carriage will pick him up.'

I decided to take Flora and meet him from the coach and Mrs Grose was pleased. She was so pleased that I was sure we would agree about everything in the future. I felt comforted and not at all uneasy. She was definitely glad I was there!

The next day, I felt a little lower in spirits. I suppose it was a natural reaction after the happiness of my arrival. I think I had probably begun to understand the difficulty of my position as I walked around the house and thought about my new circumstances. I hadn't really been prepared for the size of the house or the importance of the position and I felt a little scared as well as a little proud.

---

1. **remarkable:** 與眾不同、迷人
2. **flatter:** 奉承
3. **carried away:** 興奮

My first task was to get to know little Flora and give her the chance to find out something about me. I spent the day outside with her and she was delighted when I told her that she was the only person allowed to show me around the house. She showed it step by step and room by room and secret by secret, chatting delightfully all the time and, in half an hour, we were great friends. She was very young, but I noticed her confidence and courage as she showed me empty rooms, dark corridors and crooked[1] staircases that made me hesitate. Even at the top of an old square tower that made me feel dizzy[2], Flora's morning music, her desire to tell me so many things, helped me go on.

I have not seen Bly since the day I left it, and it would probably seem much smaller to me now that I am older and have more experience of the world. But as my little guide, with her golden hair and her blue dress danced around corners and ran down corridors, I had the idea of a storybook castle of romance. Was it a fairytale castle? No; it was a big, ugly, antique, but still comfortable house, which still had a few ancient features, although many had been replaced over the years. It was only half-used, and I imagined that we were almost as lost as a handful[3] of passengers in a great drifting[4] ship. Well, I was, strangely, at the helm[5]!

On the whole I felt less apprehensive[6], as I have said, after the first day, but the end of the day left me feeling the opposite. There was a letter for me from my employer in the evening post. It was very short, simply explaining that another letter was enclosed. The other letter was addressed to my employer, but it hadn't been opened. 'I can tell from the writing that this letter is from the headmaster and the headmaster's a terribly boring man. Read him, please; deal with him;

---

1. **crooked:** 彎曲的
2. **dizzy:** 暈眩
3. **handful:** 少許
4. **drifting:** 浮
5. **helm:** 舵
6. **apprehensive:** 焦慮

I don't want to know anything about it. Not a word. I'm off!'

The letter from the headmaster gave me a second sleepless night. I had no-one to ask for advice, and I was very upset, so I spoke to Mrs Grose. 'Miles has been expelled[1] from school.'

She gave me a strange look; then she quickly looked blank.

'After the holidays, Miles cannot go back,' I continued.

She went red. 'They won't take him back?'

'Absolutely not.'

She looked up. Her eyes filled with tears. 'What has he done?'

I hesitated; then I simply gave her the letter. She shook her head sadly. She couldn't read!

I was sorry about my mistake and I put the letter back in my pocket. 'Is he really *bad*?'

The tears were still in her eyes. 'Do the gentlemen from the school say that he is bad?'

'They give no details. They simply say that it is impossible for him to stay at the school. That means that he is harmful[2] to the other boys.'

She quickly became angry. 'Master Miles! – *him* harmful?'

Her anger was honest, and although I hadn't yet met the child, I began to feel that the idea was absurd[3].

'It's terrible', cried Mrs Grose, 'to say such cruel things! He's only just ten years old.'

'Yes, yes. It's incredible.'

'See him, Miss, first. *Then* believe it!'

I was so impatient to meet him that it was almost painful. Mrs Grose understood. 'It's like saying that the little lady is harmful. Bless her,' she added the next moment – '*look* at her!'

I turned and saw Flora. Ten minutes before, I had left her in the

---

1. expelled: 開除
2. harmful: 有害

3. absurd: 可笑的、愚蠢的

schoolroom with a sheet of white paper, a pencil and some letters to copy. She had completed her boring tasks patiently. I understood Mrs Grose's comparison and picked her up into my arms and covered her with kisses.

For the rest of the day, I watched for another opportunity of speaking to Mrs Grose, especially as I think she was trying to avoid me. I found her in the hall and put my hand on her arm to stop her from walking away. 'So, you have never known him to be bad?'

She answered honestly. 'I can't say *never*.'

I was upset again. 'Then you have known him –?'

'Yes indeed, Miss, thank God!'

On reflection, I accepted this. 'You mean that a boy who never is –?'

'Is no boy for *me*!'

I held her arm tighter. 'You like them with the spirit to be naughty?' Then, before she could answer, 'So do I! But not so that they contaminate[1] –'

'Contaminate?'

My long word confused her. I explained it. 'Corrupt.'

She stared, trying to understand my meaning; but she gave a strange laugh. 'Are you afraid he'll corrupt *you*?'

She asked the question with good humour, so I gave a silly laugh like hers.

The next day, when it was almost time to meet Miles, I spoke to Mrs Grose again. 'Tell me about the lady who was here before.'

'The last governess? She was also young and pretty – almost as young and pretty as you, Miss.'

'He seems to like us young and pretty!'

'Oh, he *did*,' Mrs Grose agreed: 'it was the way he liked everyone!'

---

1. **contaminate:** 玷污

As soon as she had spoken, she seemed to stop herself. 'I mean, that's *his* way – the master's.'

I was surprised. 'But who were you talking about first?'

She looked blank, but she coloured. 'Why, about *him*.'

'About the master?'

'Who else?'

There was no-one else, but I had the impression that she had accidentally said more than she wanted. I simply asked what I wanted to know. 'Did *she* see anything in the boy–?'

'Anything that wasn't right? She never told me.'

'Was she careful? Particular[1]?'

Mrs Grose seemed to be trying to answer honestly. 'About some things – yes.'

'But not about all?'

Again, she considered. 'Well, Miss, she's gone. I won't tell tales[2].'

'I understand completely,' I replied quickly, but decided to continue: 'Did she die here?'

'No, she went off.'

'She was taken ill, you mean, and went home?'

'She was not taken ill in this house. She left it, at the end of the year, to go home, as she said, for a short holiday. But our young lady never came back, and just as we were expecting her, I heard from the master that she was dead.'

'But what did she die of?'

'He never told me! But please, Miss,' said Mrs Grose, 'I must get back to my work.'

---

1. **particular:** 過於講究的

2. **tell tales:** 說三道四

Reading Comprehension

1 Answer the questions, true (T) or false (F). Correct the false answers.

           T   **F**

1 At the beginning of the chapter, the governess is not certain that Mrs Grose is happy to see her. ☐ ☐

_____

2 The governess thinks she hears a child's cry in the night. ☐ ☐

_____

3 Mrs Grose says that Miles is not as good-looking as his sister. ☐ ☐

_____

4 Bly is much bigger than the governess had thought. ☐ ☐

_____

5 Flora shows the governess around the house. ☐ ☐

_____

6 The governess says that Bly is a beautiful house. ☐ ☐

_____

7 Miles has been expelled from school. ☐ ☐

_____

8 Mrs Grose loves reading. ☐ ☐

_____

9 The headmaster's letter explains exactly why Miles has been expelled. ☐ ☐

_____

10 The previous governess died at Bly. ☐ ☐

_____

FCE – Writing

2 **This is part of a letter from an English-speaking friend.**

We're reading The Turn of the Screw *in class. I know you're reading it too. What do you think of the beginning? We've got as far as Chapter Two.*

Write a letter to your friend, giving your opinion. Write 120-180 words.

Vocabulary

"a hand**ful** of passengers" means a small number of passengers. As a suffix, **-ful** means the quantity that can be held in one place.

3 **Choose a logical ending for each expression from the words in the box. More than one answer may be possible.**

coins • flowers • people • paper • shopping • water

a roomful of   _____
b pocketful of   _____
c bagful of   _____
d glassful of   _____
e vaseful of   _____
f boxful of   _____

Grammar

4 **-ing or infinitive? Complete the sentences with the correct form of the verbs and then check your answers in the wordsearch.**

1 'It's like _____ that the little lady is harmful,' said Mrs Grose. (say)

2 Flora seemed _____ the governess. (like)

3 Mrs Grose avoided _____ to the governess. (talk)

4 Mrs Grose was very glad _____ the governess. (see)

5 The children's uncle sent the letter to the governess instead of _____ it himself. (read)

6 The governess felt lucky to be able _____ Flora. (teach)

7 The governess persuaded Mrs Grose _____ to her. (listen)

8 The governess told Flora _____ some exercises. (do)

9 The governess was looking forward to _____ Flora. (meet)

10 The governess wasn't used to _____ in such a big house. (live)

T	O	L	I	K	E	O	O	D	E
A	O	I	T	O	T	E	A	C	H
L	I	V	H	A	O	O	O	R	J
K	S	I	T	O	L	A	S	F	X
I	O	N	O	R	I	S	S	E	F
N	I	G	D	M	S	G	A	V	E
G	O	B	O	K	T	F	Y	L	L
M	R	E	M	E	E	T	I	N	G
R	E	A	D	I	N	G	N	R	Y
S	N	U	N	D	L	R	G	C	K

Quotations

5a "[we were] almost as lost as a handful of passengers in a great drifting ship. Well, I was, strangely, at the helm!" is one of the most famous quotations from *The Turn of the Screw*.
Can you match the following citations to the author?

William Shakespeare	a) To be or not to be, that is the question
William Wordsworth	b) Romeo, Romeo, wherefore art thou Romeo
William Blake	c) I wandered lonely as a cloud
Walt Whitman	d) O captain! my captain!
Jane Austen	e) Tyger, Tyger burning bright
William Shakespeare	f) It is a truth universally acknowledged that a single man in possession of a good fortune, must be in want of a wife.

5b Google your answers to check!

PRE-READING ACTIVITIES

Speaking

6a Are these adjectives positive (P), negative (N) or both (B)? Tick the boxes.

	P	N	B
• fresh	☐	☐	☐
• fragrant	☐	☐	☐
• innocent	☐	☐	☐
• loving	☐	☐	☐
• cunning	☐	☐	☐
• mean	☐	☐	☐
• pure	☐	☐	☐
• handsome	☐	☐	☐
• charming	☐	☐	☐
• ugly	☐	☐	☐

6b In the next chapter, the governess meets Miles for the first time. What do you think he will be like? Discuss your ideas in pairs.

Chapter Two

"Dazzled by their loveliness."

Mrs Grose had turned her back on me, but this did not stop us from liking each other, especially when we met after I had brought little Miles home. I said I was amazed and horrified that a child like him could have been expelled from school. It was monstrous.

I was a little late meeting him, and he was standing outside the inn where the coach had left him. I instantly saw the same great glow[1] of freshness and fragrance of purity, both external and internal, that I had seen in his little sister the moment I met her. He was incredibly beautiful, as Mrs Grose had suggested. I forgot everything except a passion of tenderness for him. By the time I had got back to Bly with him, I was confused and angry about the horrible letter locked up in my room in a drawer. As soon as I could find a moment for a private word with Mrs Grose, I told her the letter was grotesque[2]. She understood immediately. 'You mean the cruel accusation –?'

'It's absolutely impossible. *Look* at him!'

She smiled at the idea that I had discovered his charm. 'Yes, Miss, I do nothing else! What will you say then?' she immediately added.

'In answer to his letter?'

I had made up my mind. 'Nothing.'

1. glow: 光

2. grotesque: 荒唐

'And to his uncle?'

I was incisive. 'Nothing.'

'Then I'll stand by[1] you. We'll sort this out ourselves.'

'We'll sort it out!' I echoed passionately, giving her my hand to shake.

She held my hand for a moment, then said, 'Would you mind, Miss, if I –'

'Kissed me? No!' We embraced like sisters and still felt very indignant[2], but much stronger.

So much happened that I have to work hard now to remember how it happened. I am amazed now when I look back on the situation. With my companion, I had agreed to sort out the problem. I was acting from infatuation and pity. I was ignorant and confused, and perhaps a little conceited[3]; I thought it would be simple to deal with a boy whose education for the world was just about to begin.

But *I* learnt more than the children did. I learnt something quickly, something that had not been part of my own pathetic education. I learnt to be amused, and even amusing, and not to think too much about the future. It was the first time that I had known space and air and freedom, all the music of summer and all the mystery of nature. And then there was consideration – and consideration was sweet. It was a trap – accidental, but deep – for my imagination, perhaps for my vanity. I was calm and unworried. I didn't expect any difficulties. The children were no trouble – they were incredibly gentle. They were healthy and happy now; but almost as if they were royal princes, I had the idea that everything for them would have to be enclosed and protected, and for their futures I imagined a romantic royal extension of the park and the gardens. The change came like the pounce[4] of a wild animal.

In the first few weeks, the days were long; they often gave me what

1. **stand by:** 支持
2. **indignant:** 感到憤慨
3. **conceited:** 自滿
4. **pounce:** 跳躍

I used to call my own hour, when the children were in bed and I had a short time alone. I liked my companions very much, but this hour was the thing in the day that I liked most; especially when, as the light faded, I could walk around the gardens and enjoy the beauty and dignity of the place, almost as if it belonged to me. I felt calm and justified and I thought about how my quiet good sense was also giving pleasure to my employer – if only he thought about it! I was doing what he had asked me to do, what he had hoped I would do and the fact that I *could* do it made me happier than I expected. I thought I was a remarkable young woman. Well, I certainly needed to be remarkable to face the remarkable things which were soon to happen.

One late afternoon, the children were in bed and I had come out for my walk. One of the thoughts that I used to have as I walked around the park was as charming[1] as a charming story – that I would suddenly meet someone. Someone would appear at the corner of the path and would smile at me, with approval. I didn't ask more than that, I only wanted him to *know*; and the only way to be sure that he knew would be if I could see it in his handsome face. That face was very much in my mind when I looked up at the house. I stopped, shocked and surprised, as my daydream turned into reality. He *was* standing there! He was high up, at the very top of the tower little Flora had shown me on that first morning. My second surprise came when I realized that I had made a mistake in my first impression of the man I saw in the clear twilight[2]: he was not the person I had, at first, thought.

I was very confused. A young woman who has always lived at home is allowed to be afraid when she sees a man she doesn't know in a lonely place. I had not seen this man in Harley Street – I had not seen him anywhere.

---

1. **charming:** 迷人

2. **twilight:** 暮光

Today, simply writing my story of this meeting, I can remember how I felt. It was as if everything around me had died. And as I write, I can hear the intense silence again. The rooks stopped cawing[1] in the golden sky and the friendly hour lost its voice. There was no other change in nature: the gold was still in the sky and the air was still clear, and the man who looked at me from the tower was as definite as a picture in a frame.

I thought, with incredible speed, of all the people he might have been, but wasn't. How long did this moment last? Long enough to think of a dozen[2] possibilities. Who was this person in the house? I was in charge here, and this made me feel quite angry.

Strangely, the man wasn't wearing a hat. He seemed to stare at me. We were too far apart to speak to each other. He was standing very straight in the corner. I saw him as clearly as I can see the letters I am writing on this page; then, he slowly walked to the other corner of the tower. He was staring at me all the time. He was still staring at me as he turned away. I stood rooted to the spot[3]. Was there a secret at Bly? Did Bly have its own Gothic horror story or mad relative locked in the tower?

I don't remember how long I stayed in the garden, but it was dark when I got back to the house. In my shock, I had walked and walked. I remember going into the bright hall and meeting Mrs Grose who had been worried about me. It was clear, however, that she knew nothing at all about the incident.

It seems strange to me now, but I think the real beginning of fear came then, when I decided not to tell my companion about my encounter. I vaguely explained that I was late because the evening had been so beautiful and went to my room as soon as I could.

---

1. cawing: 發出烏鴉叫聲
2. a dozen: 十二

3. rooted to the spot: 愣在原地

Over the next few days, I thought about the incident with the man at the top of the tower. There were hours, or at least there were moments, when I had to forget my duties and think. I wasn't exactly nervous, but I was determined not to become so. The simple truth was that there was no explanation of the visitor I had met. At the end of three days, I was certain that the servants hadn't played a trick[1] on me and that no-one knew what I knew. There was only one sane[2] explanation; someone, a traveller who was curious about old houses, had come into the gardens, stood for a while to enjoy the view and then left, as quietly as he had come. The good news was, we wouldn't see him again.

I occupied myself with my charming work. My charming work was simply my life with Miles and Flora. They were a constant joy and I forgot all the concerns that I had had before I started working as a governess. The work wasn't dull, it wasn't grey, it wasn't hard. The work was charming in its daily beauty. It was all the romance of the nursery and the poetry of the schoolroom. I made constant new discoveries about my pupils, although there was one area where I made no new discoveries: I still had no idea why Miles had been expelled from school. My conclusion was that his rosy innocence was too fine and too fair for the horrid[3], unclean school world. Even headmasters could be stupid and vindictive[4].

Both children were incredibly gentle. They were almost impersonal and like little angels; it was impossible to punish them. I remember thinking that Miles, in particular, seemed to have no history. This little boy was so sensitive, yet so happy, that it was clear that he had never suffered. This meant that he had never been punished. If he had been bad, he would have been punished. He was, therefore, an angel. He never talked about school, never talked about a school friend or a teacher and

---

1. **played a trick:** 惡作劇
2. **sane:** 理智
3. **horrid:** 可怕
4. **vindictive:** 懷恨在心

I never mentioned them to him. Of course, I was under his spell[1], but I knew this, even then. I enjoyed it, it was better than thinking about the problems I read about in letters from home. Nothing in the world mattered when I was with my children, I was dazzled[2] by their loveliness.

One Sunday, it rained so hard and for so long, that we couldn't walk to church in the morning. Mrs Grose and I agreed that, if the weather got better in the evening, we would go to the late service together. The rain stopped and I got ready for my walk. Walking through the park and into the village would take about twenty minutes.

As I was coming downstairs, I remembered I had left my gloves in the dining room, so went in to get them. The day was still grey, but there was some afternoon light left. It was clear enough for me to see the gloves on a chair near the large window, but also to see a person, on the other side of the window looking straight in. I saw him immediately. The person looking straight in was the person I had seen at the top of the tower. I didn't see him more clearly than before – that was impossible – but now he was much nearer: I breathed in sharply and went cold. He was the same. His face was close to the glass. He only stayed a few seconds – long enough to show me that he saw me and recognized me; but it was as if I had been looking at him for years and had always known him. Something happened, however, that had not happened before. He stared at me, as he had before, but he also looked around at other things. He had come for someone else.

I was shocked, but the knowledge that he was not looking for me produced an extraordinary effect. I felt a sudden vibration of duty and courage. I ran out of the room and in an instant I was out of the house. I raced along the terrace around the corner and there it was – nothing. My visitor had vanished. The terrace, the lawn[3] and the garden into the

1. **spell:** 影響
2. **dazzled:** 被迷倒

3. **lawn:** 草坪

distance were empty with a great emptiness. I knew he wasn't hiding in the trees. Instinctively[1], I went to the window and looked through it, exactly as he had done. At this moment, Mrs Grose came into the room. She saw me, as I had seen my own visitor. She started[2], as I had done. She turned white, and I wondered if *I* had turned so pale. She stared, then left the room, just as I had done. I knew she was coming out of the house, to me. I stayed where I was, thinking. I wondered why *she* should be scared.

As soon as she came into view, round the corner of the house I understood why as she spoke. 'What's the matter? You're as white as a sheet.'

She was out of breath.

I considered and reached out my hand to find hers. 'I can't go to church.'

'Has anything happened?'

'Yes. Did I look strange?'

'Through the window? Terrible.'

'Well,' I said, 'I've been frightened. I saw what you saw when you came into the room. A face at the window. What *I* saw, just before, was much worse.'

Her hand tightened. 'What was it?'

'An extraordinary man. Looking in.'

---

1. instinctively: 本能地   **2. started:** 驚訝

Reading Comprehension

1 **Put these nine events into the order they appear in the story.**

1 ☐ Before leaving the house, the governess goes into the dining room.

2 ☐ The governess tells Mrs Grose about her two 'meetings' with the man.

3 ☐ One afternoon, the governess goes into the garden for a walk.

4 ☐ One Sunday, the governess and Mrs Grose decide to go to church.

5 ☐ The governess and Mrs Grose decide not to write to the children's uncle.

6 ☐ The governess meets Miles for the first time.

7 ☐ The governess runs outside to try and find the man.

8 ☐ The governess sees a man standing at the top of the tower.

9 ☐ The governess sees the man from the tower at the dining room window.

2 **Look again at the first page of Chapter Two. Find words that mean the same as the words/phrases below. The words are in the same order in the text.**

a) negatively surprised _____

b) sent away from _____

c) immediately _____

d) innocence _____

e) extremely _____

f) apart from _____

g) confidential _____

h) horribly ugly _____

i) fascination _____

j) reply _____

FCE – Grammar

3 Use of English. Complete the second sentence so that it has a similar meaning to the first sentence, using the word given. **Do not change the word given**. You must use between two and five words, including the word given.

1 She had never seen a ghost before.
first
It .... she had ever seen a ghost.

2 It was only because she looked up that she saw the ghost.
never
If she hadn't looked up .... the ghost.

3 She advised the governess to write to the children's uncle.
were
'If .... write to the children's uncle,' she said.

4 She said she would be loyal to me.
stand
'I'll .... you,' she said.

5 I wish I hadn't seen the ghost!
only
If .... the ghost!

Vocabulary

4 Idioms. Use words from the box to complete these common idiomatic phrases. Use a dictionary to help you.

fiddle • cucumber • ox • sheet • parrot • feather

1 as white as a _____
2 as strong as an _____
3 as fit as a _____
4 as sick as a _____
5 as light as a _____
6 as cool as a _____

Vocabulary

5a Phrasal verbs. Match the phrasal verbs in A to the definitions in B.

A	B
'I'll **stand by** you,' she said.	a) put in jail
We'll **sort** the problem **out** ourselves.	b) support
We **talked over** the problem for some hours.	c) accept and solve
My task was to **bring** these children **up**.	d) solve
That child should be **locked up**.	e) raise/educate
I had to **face up** to the problem.	f) discuss

5b Now write another sentence using each phrasal verb. Use a dictionary to check whether it is separable or inseparable.

a) _____

b) _____

c) _____

d) _____

e) _____

f) _____

FCE –Speaking

6 **Work in pairs. Discuss these points.**

- What's your earliest memory of childhood?
- Can you remember your first day at school?
- Can you remember your first English lesson?
- Can you remember riding a bike for the first time?
- Can you remember the first time you went swimming?
- Talk about a positive non-school learning experience.
- Talk about a negative learning experience.
- Is there anything you would like to learn in the future?

Writing

7 You and your friends would like to borrow some camera
   equipment from your school to make a short film of one of
   the scenes in Chapter Two. Choose a scene, then write a short
   description of the scene you have chosen to film. Explain your
   reasons.

PRE-READING ACTIVITIES

Listening

▶ 5 **8a** Listen to the beginning of Chapter Three. Complete the
         information about the man at the window.

Name	_____ Quint
Hair color and style	_____
Height	_____
Clothing	_____
Occupation	_____
Other information	_____
	_____
	_____

8b Now read the text to check your answers and add any other
      information you can find.

Chapter Three

"Beautiful, but infamous."

5 'Who was this man?'

'I don't know.'

'Have you seen him before?'

'Yes – once. At the top of the old tower.'

'Do you mean he's a stranger? And you didn't tell me?'

She thought for a minute. 'Was he a gentleman?'

'No.'

'Was he one of the servants or someone from the village?'

'No.'

'But if he isn't a gentleman –?'

'He's a horror. I don't know who he is.'

Mrs Grose looked around again. 'We should be at church.'

'I can't go. I can't leave *them.*'

'The children?'

I spoke boldly. 'I'm afraid of *him.*'

'Are you afraid for them?'

We looked at each other. 'Aren't you?' I replied.

'How long was the man here?'

'Till I came out to meet him.'

'*I* couldn't have come out. I would have been afraid.'

'I *was* afraid. But I came out. I have my duty.'

'What's he like?' she asked.

'He has no hat. He has red hair, very red, curly and a long face. Good features, red whiskers[1], but dark eyebrows and his eyes are sharp. He's tall, straight, active, but he's not a gentleman.'

'A gentleman? No, he's no gentleman.'

'So, you know who he is, do you?'

Mrs Grose was trying to be calm. 'Is he handsome?'

'Yes.'

'And dressed –?'

'In smart clothes, but they're not his own.'

Mrs Grose was shocked. 'They're the master's!'

'You *do* know him!'

She hesitated for a second. 'Quint!' she cried, 'Peter Quint – the master's servant. His valet[2]. 'He never wore a hat. Some of the master's clothes went missing. They were both here last year. Then the master left and Quint stayed here, alone.'

'What happened to him?'

She hesitated for a long time. 'He went too,' she finally said.

'Went where?'

Her expression was extraordinary. 'He died.'

'Died?' I almost screamed.

She was very still. 'Yes. Peter Quint is dead.'

❖ ❖ ❖

6 After this terrible event, Mrs Grose and I spent the evening together.

---

1. **whiskers:** 髯鬚　　　　2. **valet:** 男僕

We cried and prayed, we made promises to each other. We talked everything over[1]. She didn't question my sanity[2]. She was the kindest person in the world.

We agreed, that night, that we would share our doubts and fears. I already knew what I was capable of doing to protect my students; but I wondered whether my honest friend was ready to share such a terrible burden[3]. We had already gone over every detail of my encounter with Quint, but I remember how strength suddenly came to me just before we left each other to get ready for bed.

'He was looking for someone else, you say, someone else, not you?' said Mrs Grose.

'He was looking for little Miles.' I now understood everything clearly. *'That's* who he was looking for.'

'But how do you know?'

'I know, I know!' I was excited now. 'And you know too, my dear!'

She didn't deny this, she simply said, 'What will happen if *he* sees him?'

'Little Miles? That's what he wants!'

She looked very scared. 'The child?'

'Not the child. It's what *Quint* wants. He wants to appear to the children.' It was a horrible thought, but I was ready. I was absolutely certain that I would see the ghost again, but a voice inside me told me that if I was brave, if I faced the challenge, if I alone overcame it, I could save the children. I remember one of the last things I said to Mrs Grose that evening. 'It's strange that my pupils have never mentioned Quint.'

'Oh, the little girl doesn't remember. She never heard, or knew about his death.'

'Perhaps not. But Miles would remember – Miles would know.'

Mrs Grose looked afraid.

1. **talked over:** 商量
2. **sanity:** 理智

3. **burden:** 負擔、重任

'Didn't you say that Miles and Quint were "great friends"?' I continued.

'Quint liked to play with him and spoil[1] him. He was too free.'

'Too free with *my* boy?'

'Too free with everyone!'

It was midnight when I asked the question I thought was the most important. 'Was Quint definitely bad, then? Did everyone know this?'

'I didn't tell the master. He doesn't like complaints, he likes everything to run smoothly.'

'I would have told the master.'

She understood my meaning. 'I was probably wrong, but I was afraid of the things that man could do. Quint was so clever, he was so deep.'

'You weren't afraid of anything else? His effect on innocent young lives?'

'No! The master left Quint in charge here, even of *them*.'

'The children – that *creature*?' I wanted to howl[2] like an animal.

Later that night, I started to worry. Was there something Mrs Grose hadn't told me? I had been completely honest with her. But, by morning, I was convinced that there was something Mrs Grose was keeping secret, probably because she was terribly afraid. I thought about what she had said. Peter Quint had lived for months at Bly until, early one winter's morning, he had been found dead on the road leading from the village. There were injuries to his head. There had been an inquest and a lot of gossip, but it appeared that Quint had been returning to Bly from the village pub, where he had been drinking. The road had been icy and he had fallen, causing the injuries to his head. But perhaps the secrets in his life told a different story.

What effect did this ghostly appearance have on me? I was elated[3]. I was filled with joy at the heroic task before me. I had been asked for a

1. **spoil:** 縱容
2. **howl:** 嚎叫
3. **elated:** 狂喜

service, a service which was both dangerous and difficult. I myself would succeed where other girls might fail. I was there to protect and defend the most lovable, lonely little children in the world. They were helpless and I was there to serve them. We were cut off[1], united in our danger. They had nothing but me, and I had *them*. It was a magnificent chance. I was a screen; the more I saw, the less they would see. I began to watch them more closely. I was excited and if this excitement had continued too long, it might have turned to madness. What saved me from madness was proof.

One afternoon, I was alone in the gardens with Flora and we were walking in the afternoon shade. She was very like her brother. Both children were self-sufficient. They amused themselves. My task was to watch them and admire. Flora was now playing by herself on the edge of the lake, while I was sitting, mending[2], on the old stone bench[3] nearby. We had started studying geography, so in Flora's game, the lake was the Sea of Azof[4]. Suddenly, I became aware that someone was watching us from the other side of the Sea of Azof. I could sense the presence of the third person, although I didn't look up. I knew what I was going to see. There was an alien presence, someone who should not be there. My fear was that the child would see this person, this presence. Without looking across the lake, I transferred my gaze to little Flora. She was playing with a small piece of wood, thinking about making a boat. I gained strength from watching Flora's game, strength enough to do what I had to do. I lifted my eyes – I faced what I had to face.

I found Mrs Grose as soon as I could. 'The children know. It's monstrous!' I cried.

'What do you mean?'

---

1. cut off: 與世隔絕
2. mending: 修補
3. bench: 兩至三人的長椅

4. Sea of Azof: 或 Sea of Asov，黑海北面的亞速海

'Two hours ago, in the garden. Flora *saw!*'

'Did she tell you this?' Mrs Grose was horrified.

'Not a word. That's the terrible thing. That child of eight told me nothing!'

'Then how do you know?'

'I was there – I saw with my own eyes: saw that she was perfectly aware.'

'Of *him?*'

'No – of *her*. Another figure this time, just as horrific and just as evil: a woman in black, pale and dreadful – with such an air and such a face! On the other side of the lake. I was there with the child when she just appeared.'

'Was she someone you've never seen?'

'Yes, but someone the child has seen. Someone *you* have. My predecessor – the one who died.'

'Miss Jessel?'

'Miss Jessel. You don't believe me.'

'How can you be sure?'

I was impatient. 'Ask Flora – *she's* sure!' I changed my mind[1]. 'No, don't ask Flora. She'll lie. Flora doesn't want me to know.'

'Probably because she doesn't want you to be afraid.'

'No, no. The more I see, the more afraid I get.'

'Are you afraid of seeing her again?' asked Mrs Grose.

'No, I'm afraid of not seeing her. That means the child will see her and I won't know.'

Mrs Grose tried to calm me down. 'The child is innocent. She is. We must always remember that. Tell me again. How do you know it was Miss Jessel?'

---

1. **changed my mind:** 改變想法

'She didn't look at me. She stared at the child. She had such a look.'

'Was it a look of hate?'

'No, much worse. It was a look of determination. She wants the child. She wants to get Flora.'

Mrs Grose walked over to the window. After a while she turned round. 'The person was in black, you say?'

'Yes, but very beautiful. Wonderfully beautiful, but infamous[1].'

Mrs Grose spoke slowly. 'Miss Jessel *was* infamous. They were both infamous.'

I understood why Mrs Grose hadn't spoken about this before, but I needed answers. 'What did she die of? Was there something between them?'

'Yes. In spite of the difference between their status. *She* was a lady.'

I thought about Miss Jessel and the man, the servant.

Mrs Grose continued, 'I've never known anyone like him. He did what he wanted.'

'With her?'

'With all of them.'

'It must have been what *she* wished too.'

Mrs Grose's face showed that she agreed. 'Poor woman. She paid for it.'

'Then you don't know how she died?'

'No, but she couldn't stay here. A governess. It's dreadful.'

I burst into tears[2]. 'I can't save them,' I cried, 'they're lost.'

---

1. infamous: 聲名狼藉   2. burst into tears: 突然哭起來

FCE – Reading Comprehension

1 **Choose the best answer – A, B, C or D.**

1 What is Mrs Grose's reaction to the governess's story of the man?

A ☐ She is interested in finding out more about him.

B ☐ She tries to suggest that the governess imagined the man.

C ☐ She is afraid for the children.

D ☐ She is angry with the governess.

2 Who was Peter Quint?

A ☐ A friend of the children's uncle.

B ☐ Miss Jessel's brother.

C ☐ One of the children's uncle's servants.

D ☐ A traveller in the area.

3 Why is the governess surprised?

A ☐ Because Miles has never talked about Quint.

B ☐ Because Flora never liked Quint.

C ☐ Because Mrs Grose used to play with Miles.

D ☐ Because Miles didn't like Quint.

4 Who does the governess think Flora can see at the lake?

A ☐ Quint.

B ☐ Her brother.

C ☐ Miss Jessel.

D ☐ No-one.

5 How does the governess describe her predecessor?

A ☐ A woman in white, pale and dreadful.

B ☐ A woman in white, pale and beautiful.

C ☐ A woman in black, pale and ugly.

D ☐ A woman in black, pale and dreadful.

6 What does Mrs Grose suggest about Quint and Miss Jessel?

A ☐ That they had an unfortunate love affair.

B ☐ That Quint was unkind to Miss Jessel.

C ☐ That the children's uncle had an affair with Miss Jessel.

D ☐ That Quint loved Miss Jessel.

Writing

2a **Write a summary of the story so far. Consider:**
- Plot
- Action
- Characters

2b **Add your opinion about the relationship between the governess and the children.**

FCE – Grammar

3 **Use the word given in capitals at the end of some of the lines to form a word that fits in the gap in the same line.**

Essex - the location of Bly	
Essex is a county in the southeast of England. The main **1** _____ headquarters are in the town of Chelmsford. The countryside is quite	**ADMINISTRATION**
flat and marshy, especially in **2** _____ areas. Stansted airport is **3** _____	**COAST**
	LOCATION
in Essex. Some **4** _____ seaside resorts	**INTEREST**
include Clacton and Southend. Important industries are **5** _____ and food	**ENGINEER**
6 _____.	**PROCESS**

Vocabulary

4 **Adjective Wordsearch. There are ten adjectives from Chapter Three in this wordsearch. Find the adjectives and match them to the definitions below.**

1 an opposite of ugly. _____

2 describes the clothes you wear on an important occasion. _____

3 describes a person who is helpful/nice to you. _____

4 a synonym for afraid. _____

5 a synonym for pure. _____

6 when temperatures are low, roads are often like this. _____

7 brave, someone who deserves admiration. _____

8 a synonym for notorious. _____

9 means the same as conscious. _____

10 an ill person, or a person who has had a shock is often this colour. _____

B	O	S	I	H	A	O	O	D	E
A	E	C	T	O	E	W	A	C	H
S	M	A	R	T	O	R	A	R	J
K	P	R	U	I	C	Y	O	R	X
I	A	E	O	T	I	S	S	I	E
N	L	D	D	M	I	G	A	V	C
D	E	B	O	K	T	F	Y	L	L
M	I	N	F	A	M	O	U	S	G
I	N	N	O	C	E	N	T	L	Y
S	N	U	N	Y	L	R	G	C	K

5a **Reported speech. Put these direct sentences into reported speech.**

1 "I don't know this man."
She said _____

2 "He is handsome."
She said _____

3 "They were both here last year."
She remembered _____

4 "The master left Quint in charge."
She said _____

5b **Now do the same with these direct questions. Remember: the word order is the same as for affirmative sentences.**

1 "Did Flora tell you this?"
She asked whether _____

2 "How do you know?"
She asked _____

3 "How can you be sure?"
She asked _____

PRE-READING ACTIVITY

Speaking

6 **Read the quotations from the next chapter and discuss the questions in pairs.**

1 "I decided to see if I could get more information about his [Miles's] bad behaviour."
a) What do you think the governess found out about Miles?
b) Is Miles really bad, or is he a normal child?

2 "My candle went out, but even without it, in the early morning light, I saw someone on the stairs."
a) Who do you think the governess saw on the stairs?
b) What do you think she did?

3 "The first thing I saw […] was that Flora's little bed was empty."
a) Where do you think Flora was?
b) What did the governess do?

Chapter Four

"Innocent and doomed."

Late that night, while the house slept, Mrs Grose and I had another talk; she told me that she had no doubts about what I had seen. I explained that it was impossible for me to have made the things up[1], especially since she had been the one to recognize the ghosts from my descriptions. She didn't really want to talk about it, but we agreed that I should be careful, that I should expect to see them again. My real concern, at this stage, was my new suspicion. I was suspicious of Flora.

After my first talk with Mrs Grose, I had, of course, returned to the children. I had gone straight back to Flora's special company and she had noticed that I had been crying. It was terrible to look into those deep beautiful eyes and think that they were cunning[2]. It was impossible: their voices, their pressure on my heart, and their fragrant faces made it seem impossible. They were innocent and beautiful. I didn't want to think about Flora by the lake, I didn't want to ask her about the vision. I tried to convince myself that she hadn't seen Miss Jessel.

I was also aware that it had been necessary to push Mrs Grose for information. She had told me a great deal, but bit-by-bit and under pressure. When Miles had been expelled from school, she had said that she couldn't say that Miles had *never* been bad. I decided to see

1. **made things up:** 編故事   2. **cunning:** 狡猾

if I could get more information about his 'bad' behaviour. Mrs Grose simply told me that Quint and the boy had been together all the time, for months. She herself had even talked to Miss Jessel about it. Miss Jessel had reacted very strangely and had told Mrs Grose to mind her own business[1], so she had spoken directly to little Miles.

'What did you say to him?' I asked.

'I reminded the boy that Quint was a servant. He denied spending time with Quint. This was a lie. Sometimes it was as if Quint was his tutor and Miss Jessel was Flora's, they spent so much time together.'

'So the boy hid their relationship.'

'But, if he was so bad then, and so bad at school, how can he be such an angel now?'

'I don't know,' I cried. I asked whether Miles had spoken rudely to Mrs Grose. After all, Mrs Grose was a servant too. She agreed that he had, but that she had forgiven him.

'Still,' I said, 'in any case, while Miles was with the man, Flora was with the woman, and that suited them all.' I made my final observation to Mrs Grose. 'Miles lied and was impudent[2], but this is quite natural. I am determined, however, to watch them both.'

'Surely you don't think that he sees Quint?'

'No, I accuse him of nothing. Until I get further evidence, I must wait.' I left the room.

❖ ❖ ❖

I waited and the days made me calmer. Sometimes, my contact with the children seemed to make the previous incidents fade into the background. I was able to surrender to their childish grace. I wondered whether they guessed that I was thinking strange things

---

1. to mind her own business: 別多管閒事   **2. impudent:** 無禮

about them; I was afraid of them seeing how interesting I thought they were – innocent and doomed[1]. Often, I found myself taking the children into my arms and kissing them. As soon as I had done this, I would say to myself: 'What will they think of that? Am I showing too much emotion?' It would have been easy to go mad in such circumstances, but I could still enjoy the charm of my companions, despite my fear that their charm was a mask. I remember thinking that their behaviour was a little strange in the way they were showing me *more* affection.

I didn't find their affection for me false. They wanted to do everything for their poor governess. They understood their lessons better and better, which satisfied me; they read to me and acted and told me stories; they learnt passages by heart to please me. Studying had always come naturally to them. They loved their work and they both had excellent memories. I was happy with everything, except Miles and school. I didn't want to think about it, but I knew that Miles was too clever for a bad governess, for a parson's daughter, to spoil. It was a mystery why he had been expelled from school, but it was easy to delay his departure for a new one.

I was now very concerned to make sure that I was always with the children. We lived in a cloud of music and love and success and private theatricals. The children were very good at music, especially Miles, who often played the schoolroom piano. Flora adored her brother and, as I had brothers myself, I knew that little girls often loved little boys slavishly[2]. But this little boy was extraordinary in the way he looked after his sister. They never quarrelled or complained. They understood each other so well, that sometimes one would keep me busy while the other one slipped away[3].

---

1. doomed: 不幸
2. slavishly: 奴隶似地

3. slipped away: 溜走

I am delaying too much, but that is because I am renewing my suffering as I write this. Now I must move on with the story.

One evening, unexpectedly, I felt the cold touch of the impression I had had on the night of my arrival. I was not yet in bed, but I was reading by the light of a couple of candles. I remember being totally awake and that it was very late indeed. I can still see Flora's bed today, enclosed in its white draperies[1], as the little girl lay sleeping. I don't know why, but I suddenly found myself looking at the door. I listened, remembering the sensation I had had on my first night of someone moving around the house. I felt a soft breeze coming through the window.

It seems incredible to me now, but my courage was magnificent. I got up, picked up a candle and walked out of the room, then closed and locked the door behind me. I don't know what guided me, but I walked straight along, until I came to the tall window at the turn of the staircase. I was aware of three things at once. They were simultaneous, although they had flashes of succession. My candle went out, but even without it, in the early morning light, I saw someone on the stairs. Quint. The apparition was halfway up the stairs. It stopped when it saw me and stared at me, exactly as it had from the tower and from the garden. He knew who I was, just as well as I knew who he was. So, in the cold, faint light we faced each other. He was, on this occasion, a living, detestable[2], dangerous presence. But, wonder of wonders, I was not afraid.

He knew I was not terrified and I was full of confidence as I stood there in front of him. The thing was as real and as horrible as if it were human: horrible because it *was* human, like meeting alone, in the small hours, in a sleeping house, some enemy, some adventurer, some criminal. The dead silence and our nearness was the only

---

1. draperies: 布簾

2. detestable: 面目可憎

unnatural horror. If I had met a murderer in such a place, at such a time, at least we would have spoken. The silence was witness to my strength as the figure disappeared. I saw it turn, like a servant obeying an order, and go straight down the staircase into the darkness.

I returned to my room. The first thing I saw, by the light of the remaining candle, was that Flora's little bed was empty; now I felt all the terror I had not felt five minutes before. I pulled back the draperies, then I heard a sound: the drapes at the window moved and the child came out, pink like a rose, from behind them. She stood there in her nightdress, with her pink bare feet and the golden glow of her curls. She looked serious as she said, in a change of roles, 'You naughty thing, where *have* you been?'

I found myself explaining. And she herself explained why she was out of bed, with lovely simplicity. She said she had known, as she lay in bed, that I had left the room and had got up to look for me. I sat down in my chair and she sat in my arms, the candle glowing in her wonderful little face. 'Did you think I was walking in the garden?'

'I thought someone was,' she replied.

'Did you see anyone?'

'Oh, *no!*' she returned, innocently.

At that moment, I absolutely believed she was lying; I closed my eyes to think while I held on to the little girl tightly. I wanted to tell her straight, tell her lovely little lighted face. But, I couldn't, so I simply asked. 'Why did you pull the draperies across to make me think you were still in bed?'

Flora luminously[1] considered then smiled, divinely, 'Because

---

1. **luminously:** 聰明地

I didn't want to frighten you.' She looked at the candle, as if the question were irrelevant. I put her back to bed.

You can imagine what my nights were like from that moment. I sat up till late, I waited until Flora was asleep and regularly crept[1] out of my room looking for Quint. I never met him there again; I never saw him in the house again.

Once, on the staircase, I had a different adventure. Looking from the top, I saw a woman sitting on one of the lower stairs. Her back was to me and her head, in deep sadness, was in her hands. She vanished[2] without looking at me.

I had plenty of other opportunities for bravery. On the eleventh night after I had met Quint's ghost – I was counting now – I had a terrible shock. It was the first night that I had been to bed at my normal time and I had fallen asleep immediately. I woke up suddenly at about one o'clock. I had left a candle burning, but it had gone out. I was certain that Flora had put it out. I got up, in the darkness, and went to her bed. It was empty. I looked at the window, there she was. She had got up again, had blown out the candle and was looking out into the night. She hadn't heard me and she didn't respond when I lit the candle with a match. She was watching the garden by the light of the moon. I was sure she was face-to-face with the apparition we had met at the lake and could now communicate with it. I had to get to another window, without disturbing her: I had to see. I went out of the room silently, and listened at the door. She hadn't heard me. I stood in the corridor, looking at her brother's door. I had a strong impulse – what if I went into his room and walked straight over to *his* window? I went over to his door, stopped and listened. I wondered if his bed would be empty too and if he were secretly watching as well.

1. crept: 爬出   2. vanished: 消失

I waited for a minute. He was quiet, he might be innocent, the risk was too great and I turned away.

I was sure there was a figure in the garden – the visitor Flora was watching: but I didn't think it was the visitor most closely connected to the boy. There were many empty rooms at Bly and I decided to go into the old tower from where I could see the garden and Flora's room. I went into the large, square room at the corner. I crossed this chill[1] room and opened the blind[2], as quietly as I could. I could see the garden and I saw something else. In the moonlight, I could see a figure standing still, fascinated, looking up to where I was standing, or at least, to something directly above me. There was clearly another person above me, at the top of the tower. The presence on the lawn was not what I had expected – I felt ill. The person on the lawn was poor little Miles himself.

---

1. **chill:** 寒冷   2. **blind:** 窗簾

Reading Comprehension

1 **Who did/said these things in Chapter Four?**

Choose from: **A** Flora

                          B Miles

                          C The governess

                          D Mrs Grose

Which person:

1 ☐ became suspicious of Flora?

2 ☐ said she had spoken to Miss Jessel about Quint?

3 ☐ spoke rudely to Mrs Grose?

4 ☐ said she had no evidence against Miles?

5 ☐ thought that Miles was very clever?

6 ☐ played the piano very well?

7 ☐ looked after Flora?

8 ☐ met the ghost of Quint on the stairs?

9 ☐ thought that Flora was lying to her?

10 ☐ saw the ghost of a woman on the stairs?

11 ☐ said she didn't want to frighten the governess?

12 ☐ went into the garden alone at night?

Vocabulary

2 **Use your dictionary to help you. Which of these is the odd one out? Give your reasons.**

1 a ☐ fragrance **b** ☐ scent   **c** ☐ perfume   **d** ☐ stink

2 a ☐ tutor   **b** ☐ teacher **c** ☐ groom   **d** ☐ governess

3 a ☐ sunset   **b** ☐ twilight **c** ☐ dusk   **d** ☐ dawn

4 a ☐ cold   **b** ☐ chill   **c** ☐ warm   **d** ☐ frozen

5 a ☐ luminous **b** ☐ light   **c** ☐ bright   **d** ☐ gloomy

Grammar

3a Adjectives and prepositions. Complete these sentences with a preposition from the box.

to • on • of • for • at • of

1 The governess was very proud _____ not contacting the children's uncle.
2 Mrs Grose was ready _____ believe the governess.
3 Miles was very good _____ playing the piano.
4 The governess was suspicious _____ the children's behavior.
5 She was responsible _____ looking after the children.
6 The children were keen _____ acting.

3b Write true sentences about yourself using the following adjectives and prepositions. Remember that you need the *–ing* form if you follow a preposition with a verb.

- confused about _____
- tired of _____
- interested in _____
- opposed to _____

Writing

4 What do you think about the governess? Does she really see the ghosts or is she going mad? Give your opinion, using evidence from the story.

5 **Read this summary of the story so far and decide which answer (A, B, C or D) best fits each gap.**

The main action in *The Turn of the Screw* is **(1)** _____ in Bly, a house in the English countryside. The story **(2)** _____ two orphaned children, Flora and Miles who are being looked **(3)** _____ by a new governess. Most of the story is told from the governess's point of **(4)** _____. The governess is young and it is her first job, as well as her first time away from home. The governess is very protective of the children. She **(5)** _____ sees them as beautiful and innocent, although later she begins to be suspicious of them.

The main **(6)** _____ for her suspicion is that she believes they are communicating with the spirits of two people: their former governess and a servant, both of whom are dead. The governess and Mrs Grose, the housekeeper at Bly, talk about these events, **(7)** _____ Mrs Grose has not seen the spirits herself. At this stage of the story, the governess is sleeping very badly and is disturbed by **(8)** _____ meetings with the ghosts.

1 A set	**B** made	**C** happened	**D** done
2 A relates	**B** narrates	**C** involves	**D** tells
3 A for	**B** at	**C** after	**D** over
4 A opinion	**B** view	**C** look	**D** attitude
5 A lately	**B** principally	**C** once	**D** initially
6 A reason	**B** purpose	**C** target	**D** aim
7 A since	**B** spite	**C** despite	**D** although
8 A common	**B** usual	**C** often	**D** frequent

Grammar

6 **Conjunctions. Complete the sentences with a conjunction from the box. More than one answer is sometimes possible.**

> although • despite • in spite of • so • in case • even though

1 Mrs Grose had spoken to Miles _____ Miss Jessel's anger.
2 The governess walks towards the ghost _____ she is afraid.
3 The governess doesn't go to church _____ the ghost comes for Miles.
4 The governess describes the ghost _____ Mrs Grose recognizes him.
5 The governess accepted the job at Bly _____ her doubts.
6 Mrs Grose defends Miles _____ he has been expelled.

PRE-READING ACTIVITIES

Speaking

7a **Four of the following things happen in Chapter Five. Which? Tick the boxes.**

1 ☐ The governess gets extremely angry with Miles.
2 ☐ Miles explains why he went into the garden at night.
3 ☐ Flora walks in her sleep.
4 ☐ Mrs Grose sees one of the ghosts.
5 ☐ Mrs Grose suggests writing to the children's uncle.
6 ☐ The governess writes to the children's uncle.
7 ☐ The governess threatens Mrs Grose.
8 ☐ Miles says he wants to go back to school.
9 ☐ The governess sends Miles to a new school.

7b **Work in pairs. Compare your answers, giving reasons for your choices.**

Chapter Five

"When I'm bad, I am bad."

The next afternoon, I told Mrs Grose everything. She believed me, I was absolutely sure. She had no imagination at all – such a blessing[1]. She could see only beauty, amiability[2], happiness and cleverness in the children. She was serene[3], with a steady fireside glow.

We were on the terrace in the later afternoon sun, while the children were walking together on the lawn. Miles was reading a story to his sister. I told Mrs Grose about all the events of the night before. I explained that I had gone downstairs to bring Miles inside, instead of waking everyone in the house. As soon as I had appeared on the terrace, the boy had come straight to meet me; I had taken his hand and led him through the house, up the staircase where Quint had looked for him, along the landing and into his room. Miles and I hadn't spoken. I wondered how he was going to explain. He could no longer pretend to be innocent. I remember that, as we went into his small room, where the light of the moon was so bright, I sat on his bed. What could I do? Could I ask him directly? No. But I had to ask something. 'Tell me the truth now. Why did you go out?'

I can still see his wonderful smile, his beautiful eyes and his white teeth. 'If I tell you why, will you understand?'

1. blessing: 幸事
2. amiability: 友善親切
3. serene: 平靜

I nodded[1]. The little fairy prince was gentle. 'I wanted you to do this.'

'Do what?'

'Think that I was *bad*. Just once.'

He was so sweet, so happy. He kissed me. I tried hard not to cry as I held him in my arms. He was so clever – I was filled with admiration. I could do nothing, I had to accept his explanation. 'When did you go down?'

'At midnight. When I'm bad, I *am* bad.'

'I see, it's charming. But how could you be sure that I would find out?'

'I arranged it with Flora.' His answers were all ready. 'Her job was to get up and look out.'

'She did.'

'She disturbed you, and to see what she was looking at, you also looked, you saw.'

'While you were getting cold in the night air!'

He was radiant. 'It was the only way I could be really bad.' We embraced again and I left him, sure that he had deep reserves of goodness.

'I have watched them and I have waited,' I continued to Mrs Grose. 'They have *never* mentioned either Quint or Miss Jessel and Miles has never mentioned why he was expelled from school. We sit and watch them, they show off[2] to us. We think they're lost in a fairy tale, but they're really talking about *them*. They're talking about the horrors. I now understand much more.'

Mrs Grose was very still. She was staring at the children from the terrace. 'What do you now understand?'

'Their beauty, their goodness – it's just a game. They aren't being good, they're just being absent. It's easy to live with them, because they're in their own world. They're his and they're hers!'

---

1. **nodded:** 點頭

2. **show off:** 賣弄

'Quint's and that woman's?'

'Yes. They want to get them.'

'But how? Why?' Poor Mrs Grose studied the children.

'Evil. The evil they put into the children in those terrible days. They want to bring more evil.'

Mrs Grose was silent. Then she said, 'Quint and Miss Jessel *did* behave badly. But what can they do now?'

'Do?' The children looked up and smiled at us. 'They can destroy *them*!'

Mrs Grose clearly didn't understand, so I explained further. 'The ghosts are trying to destroy the children. The ghosts are trying to get nearer. At the moment, they seem to be across and beyond. They're at the top of the tower and across the lake and on the outside of windows, but I'm sure there's a plan. They are tempting the children.'

'Do they want the children to come?' asked Mrs Grose slowly.

'Or die!' Mrs Grose stood up. 'Unless we can prevent it,' I added.

Mrs Grose was standing in front of me. 'Their uncle must prevent it. He must take them away.'

'I can't write to him and tell him that his house is poisoned and that his niece and nephew are mad.'

'But what if they *are*, Miss?'

'I can't tell him this. He had one condition at the start of our contract: I must not bother him.'

Mrs Grose considered my answer. 'Make him come to you.'

I stared. 'Come to *me*?' I was suddenly afraid of what Mrs Grose might do.

'He ought to *be* here – he ought to help.'

I got up quickly. Mrs Grose didn't understand. She couldn't see what I could see: his derision[1], his amusement, his contempt. She didn't understand – no-one did – how proud I was to serve him, not to break his condition. I decided to warn her. 'If you decide to tell him –'

She was really frightened. 'Yes, Miss?'

'I will leave, immediately. I will leave him, and you.'

❖ ❖ ❖

Talking to the children was even more difficult than before and this situation continued for about a month. I was also sure that my pupils knew I was worried. I am as sure today as I was then, that this was not in my imagination. Of course, they didn't say anything to me; they would never do anything like that. But we often found that we had to change the course of our conversations to avoid mentioning certain things. It was like opening the wrong door and having to shut it quickly, with a bang. All roads lead to Rome, and it sometimes seemed like all conversations or all school subjects led to forbidden[2] ground. I found myself talking more and more about my early life, about even the smallest adventures I had had and that my brothers and sisters and cat and dog had had. The only possible topics of conversation involved *my* life, *my* past and *my* friends. They often asked me to repeat stories about things I had already told them.

Yes, things were getting more and more difficult, although I hadn't met either of the ghosts for some time. Since the time I had seen the woman on the stairs, I hadn't seen Miss Jessel or Quint, although I expected to meet them practically every time I turned a corner.

The summer had turned and darker autumn had arrived at Bly. The grey sky, empty spaces and dead leaves made the garden look like a theatre after the performance – the floor covered with crumpled playbills[3]. The

1. **derision:** 嘲笑
2. **forbidden:** 禁止的
3. **playbills:** 戲單

air, the stillness, strange impressions and feelings made me think about the time I had first seen Quint in June. I recognized the signs and the portents[1].

I was obsessed. Sometimes, I was sure that the children were communicating with Quint and Miss Jessel, even when I was with them, watching them. I wanted to scream at them. 'They're here, I know they're here and you can't deny it now!' But I didn't. Sometimes, in the quiet of my room, I practised saying it to them, although I never said their names. I was silent, as they were silent. In the schoolroom, I chattered[2] about nothing. My chatter began to be broken by strange silences, still moments. This was when the others, the outsiders, were there. We could not talk about it, but the children were incredible. They were always ready with a question to help the moment pass, or one or other of them would kiss me. I knew that, whatever I had seen, Miles and Flora had seen worse and *more*.

A question they often asked was, 'When do you think he will come?' or 'Don't you think we ought to write?' *He*, of course, was their uncle and they hoped that he would come soon to join us. He never wrote to them and I made sure that the children's letters never reached him. I remembered my task; I had to stop him from being bothered, even by the children. I told the children that the letters were too beautiful to be posted and I kept them. I still have them today. This didn't stop the children from asking about their uncle, as if they knew it would be difficult for me if he came. In spite of my tension and the children's victory, however, I never lost patience with them.

Relief finally came: the relief that a thunderstorm brings to a suffocating[3] day. It was change, and it came with a rush.

---

1. portents: 預兆
2. chattered: 喋喋不休

3. suffocating: 令人窒息的

❖ ❖ ❖

We were on our way to church one Sunday morning, I was walking with Miles and his sister was ahead of us with Mrs Grose. There was a touch of frost in the air and the church bells seemed almost happy. I was thinking about my pupils. I was like a jailer[1], constantly looking for possible surprises and ways of escape. In his expensive Sunday clothes, Miles was a fine little gentleman and if he had tried to rebel, I would not have been able to stop him. I was wondering what I would do when the inevitable revolution came. It came on this crisp, clear Sunday, when, during the walk, Miles said, charmingly, 'Look, my dear, when am I going back to school?'

He had a sweet voice. He talked as if he were throwing roses. I stopped walking. There was something new between us and all that he needed to do was simply be charming. I was silent and he continued. 'A boy can't be with a lady always, my dear!' It was so respectfully easy. 'I am getting older.'

'Yes, you're getting older.'

I felt helpless and I still think, to this day, that he seemed to know and to play with the idea. 'And I have been very good, haven't I?'

'Not always, Miles.'

'There was just that one night, when I went into the garden!'

'Yes, but I can't remember why you did it.'

'I did it to show you I could!'

We started walking again and he put his hand on my arm. 'Then when *am* I going back to school?'

I put on my most responsible manner. 'Were you very happy there?'

He thought for a minute. 'I'm happy anywhere!'

1. **jailer:** 獄卒

'Well, if you're happy here –'

'Yes, but I want to see more life.'

'I see.'

We had arrived at church and I wanted to get inside before the discussion developed: inside he would have to be silent for an hour. Just before we arrived at the door, Miles almost shouted. 'I want to be with people like me!'

'There aren't many people like you, except for Flora,' I laughed.

'Are you comparing me to a baby girl?'

'Don't you love our little Flora?'

'If I didn't –'

He pulled my arm and we stopped again. Everyone had gone into church and we were alone in the churchyard[1].

'Yes, if you didn't?'

'Well, you know!'

He didn't move, but he suddenly said something which made me sit on a low, flat tomb[2]. 'Does my uncle think what *you* think?'

'How do you know what I think?'

'I don't. You never tell me. Does he know?'

'Know what, Miles?'

'How I'm doing.'

There was nothing I could say without sacrificing my employer. 'I don't think he cares much.'

Miles stood looking at me. 'He has to care. He has to come down here. *I'll* make him.'

With that, Miles ran into church.

---

1. **churchyard:** 教堂墓地　　　　2. **tomb:** 墳墓

Reading Comprehension

1 **Answer the questions about Chapter Five.**

   1 Why does Miles say he went into the garden?

   _____

   2 According to the governess, who is controlling the children?

   _____

   3 Why is the governess afraid of Mrs Grose?

   _____

   4 What season is it now?

   _____

   5 What question does Miles ask the governess?

   _____

   6 What does the governess tell Miles about his uncle?

   _____

Speaking

2a **Read the different opinions about the governess. Which do you agree with most?**

                                                          agree   disagree

   1 "She's definitely over-protective of the children, especially Miles." ☐ ☐

   2 "She's very volatile, perhaps even unstable." ☐ ☐

   3 "She just wants to help the children." ☐ ☐

   4 "The ghosts are real. She definitely sees them." ☐ ☐

   5 "The governess is mad." ☐ ☐

   6 "The ghosts are in her imagination. She's neurotic." ☐ ☐

   7 "The governess is a heroine. She's fighting to save the children." ☐ ☐

2b **Work in pairs to discuss your answers. Give reasons for your opinions.**

Grammar

3a **Modal Verbs. Match the sentence in Box A with a meaning from Box B.**

A	B
a) He ought to be here! b) He must come here! c) He needn't come here! d) He has to come here! e) He doesn't need to come here! f) He mustn't come here!	It is not necessary There is no alternative It's his duty

3b **Choose the correct alternative to make these sentences true to the text.**

1 Mrs Grose thinks the governess _____ (ought to/needn't) write to the uncle.

2 She also thinks the uncle _____ (must/doesn't need) to take the children away.

3 The governess tells Mrs Grose she _____ (mustn't/has to) tell the uncle.

4 The children think they _____ (ought to/mustn't) write to their uncle.

5 Miles says his uncle _____ (has to/needn't) come to Bly.

4 **Make and Let. Complete the sentences with the correct form of** *make* **for obligation or** *let* **for permission.**

1 The governess _____ Mrs Grose keep quiet.

2 The governess won't _____ the children talk about the past.

3 Miles _____ the governess listen to him.

4 The governess _____ Miles go into church alone.

5 The governess doesn't _____ the children study hard.

6 The children _____ the governess talk about her past.

7 Mrs Grose _____ the governess make all the important decisions.

5a **Work in pairs to discuss these pictures. They show different possible alternatives for Miles's education.**

First, talk about the advantages and disadvantages of each of these alternatives. Then decide which two would be best for Miles.

5b **What type of school did you go to? Talk about your schools to each other.**

Vocabulary

6 **Three-part Phrasal Verbs. Read the dictionary definitions then complete the sentences with the correct three-part phrasal verbs.**

look forward to = feel happy about something that is going to happen
put up with = accept behavior or a situation
stand up for = defend yourself or someone else
look back on = think about something that happened in the past

1 The governess was not _____ her next encounter with the ghosts.
2 Miles did not want to _____ being educated at home for much longer.
3 The governess is _____ her past experiences as a governess at Bly.
4 Miles _____ himself by arguing with the governess.

PRE-READING ACTIVITY

Listening

▶ 7 **7** **Listen to the beginning of Chapter Six. Are these statements true or false?**

	T	F
1 The governess follows Miles into church.	☐	☐
2 The governess thinks her relationship with Miles has broken down.	☐	☐
3 The governess walks back to Bly through the park.	☐	☐
4 The governess sits down at the dining table.	☐	☐
5 Miss Jessel's ghost is sitting in the schoolroom.	☐	☐
6 Miss Jessel's ghost screams at the governess.	☐	☐
7 Miss Jessel's ghost disappears down the stairs.	☐	☐
8 The governess decides she must stay at Bly.	☐	☐

Chapter Six

"Dear little Miles."

▶7 I didn't follow Miles into church. I sat for a while on the tomb and thought about what the boy had said. Miles now understood something; he understood that I was afraid of something. He knew I was afraid of talking to him about his expulsion[1] from school, because that was part of the horror. By now, I should really have been thinking of writing to the boy's uncle, but I didn't want to face the ugliness and pain of that. The boy was right. He had given me a choice; either resolve the problem of his expulsion with his uncle or send him to a new school. Miles understood this and he had a plan. I walked around the church, conscious that our relationship could not be repaired. For the first time since I had met him, I wanted to get away from him. This was my chance, no-one could stop me. I could get away, at least for a few hours, perhaps for longer.

I went back through the park. By the time I had reached the house, I had decided to leave. It was a quiet Sunday, which gave me the opportunity to leave without a word to anyone. But there was a problem with transport. Tormented, I sat down at the bottom of the stairs, until I remembered, horrified, that it was exactly where, a month ago, in the darkness of the night, I had seen the ghost of that horrible woman. I

---

1. expulsion: 開除，expel的名詞

jumped up and ran up the stairs into the schoolroom to collect my possessions. There, in the clear noonday light, I saw a person sitting at my table. She held her tired head in her hands, but I didn't mistake her for a maid writing a love letter to her sweetheart. I knew exactly who she was. Then she stood up, not as if she had heard me, but as if she needed to stand. My horrid predecessor was standing not far from me, melancholy[1], indifferent[2] and detached. There she was, dishonoured and tragic; but as I stared, the terrible image began to pass away. Dark as midnight in her black dress, beautiful and sorrowful, she had looked at me long enough to say that it was her right to sit at my table. While these moments lasted, I felt like the intruder. 'You terrible, miserable woman!' I heard myself scream to the empty house. She looked at me as if she heard me. The next minute, there was nothing in the room except sunshine and a sense that I had to stay at Bly.

❖❖❖

 8 I expected my pupils to say something to me when they came back from church. They said nothing, which upset me again. I looked at Mrs Grose's strange face. I was sure that the children had told her to keep silent; a silence that I decided to break as soon as possible. I managed to speak to her for five minutes, just before tea in the housekeeper's room, where she was sitting in front of the fire. I can still see her there: in her tidy, clean room with its locked drawers. 'Yes, they asked me to say nothing. What happened to you?'

'I only went with you all for the walk. I came back to meet a friend.'
She was surprised. 'A friend?'
'But did the children give you a reason?'
'Yes. They said you would prefer it. Do you?'

---

1. **melancholy:** 憂鬱   2. **indifferent:** 冷漠

'No. Did they say why I would prefer it?'

'No. Master Miles said that we needed to do everything you wanted.'

'Flora?'

'Miss Flora was so sweet. She said "Of course!" and I said the same.'

'I have spoken to Miles.'

'But what did you say, Miss?'

'Everything. It doesn't matter. I came home for a talk with Miss Jessel.'

'Did she speak? What did she say?' exclaimed Mrs Grose, shocked.

'That she suffers torments of the lost and the damned and she wants Flora to share them.' I held onto Mrs Grose. 'It doesn't matter, though. I have decided.'

'Decided what?'

'I have decided to write to their uncle.'

'Oh Miss, please do,' my friend cried.

'I will, I *will*! It's the only way. Yes. His uncle will come here and speak to the boy. It's not my fault that there's been a problem with school. I'll explain everything to his uncle. I'll show him.'

'Show him what?'

'The letter from the old school. I'll tell him I can't solve this problem because the boy's been expelled for wickedness[1].'

'We don't know why he was expelled.' Mrs Grose declared.

'What else can there be? He's clever and beautiful and perfect. Is he stupid? Is he ill? Is he bad-tempered? No, he's exquisite[2] – so it can only be that he's wicked. It's their uncle's fault. He left the children with those people.'

'He didn't really know them. It's my fault.' She had gone very pale.

'I won't let you suffer,' I answered.

---

1. wickedness: 邪惡　　　　　　　　**2. exquisite:** 出類拔萃

'I won't let the children suffer,' she emphatically[1] returned.

'Very well, I'll write. I'll write tonight,' I said as I left.

I started the letter in the evening. The weather had changed and it was windy outside, and I sat in my room, where Flora was sleeping, listening to the wind and the rain. After some time, I went out, taking a candle, and listened at Miles's door. I was listening for evidence that he was not asleep and eventually I heard some.

'Hello, come on in!' He called.

It was like joy in the darkness! I went in.

'What are *you* doing?' he said sociably.

'How did you know I was there?' I asked.

'I heard you. It sounded like an army of soldiers!' He held his hand out to me.

'Why are you awake?' I said.

'I was thinking about this strange thing between us.'

'What strange thing, Miles?'

His hand was cool. 'The way you bring me up and everything!'

I could see, by the light of the candle, that he was smiling. 'You will definitely be going back to school. But not to the old place. We must find a better school. I didn't realize that you wanted to go back, you've never talked about school.'

'Haven't I?'

My heart was aching. His little brain was puzzled. He couldn't act innocence and consistency.

'No, never. You've never talked about your teachers, your school friends or anything that happened to you at school. In fact, today was

1. **emphatically:** 強調地

the first time I have heard you talk about your past. You usually seem so happy in the present.' He was just like an adult – poisoned by *their* influence. 'I thought you wanted to stay here, at Bly.'

He coloured slightly and shook his head. 'I don't. I want to get away.'

I took temporary refuge. 'Do you want to go to your uncle?'

His sweet ironic face looked at me. 'My uncle must come down here and you must agree everything completely.'

'If we do, you will be taken away.'

'That's what I've been working for. I'll have a lot to tell him.' He was exultant.

'You, Miles, will have a lot to tell him. There are things he'll ask you.'

'What?'

'Things you've never told me. He can't send you back –'

'I don't want to go back!' He interrupted. 'I want to go somewhere else.'

He was serene and innocently happy. It was tragic to think that he would probably be back home, after three months at a new school, still the same, but with even more dishonour. It made me sad so I let myself go and embraced him. 'Dear little Miles, dear little Miles!'

My face was close to his and he let me kiss him, indulging me. 'Well, old lady?'

'Is there nothing you want to tell me?'

He turned his face away. 'I told you this morning.'

I was sorry for him. 'What do you want me to do?'

'Leave me alone,' he replied gently.

I stood up and something made me stay by his side for a moment. I didn't want to abandon him, or lose him, either. 'I've just started a letter to your uncle.'

'Well then, finish it!'

I waited. 'What happened before?'

He looked up at me. 'Before what?'

'Before you came back. Before you left school.'

He was silent. I fell to my knees. 'Dear little Miles, dear little Miles, I just want to help you! Help me to save you!'

I knew immediately that I had gone too far. There was an extraordinary chill, a gust of frozen air and the room shook as if the window had been blown out[1]. The boy gave a loud cry which could either have been jubilation[2] or terror. I jumped up and realized that the room was dark. But it was strange, the window was closed and the draperies were still. 'The candle's gone out!' I cried.

'I blew it out, my dear!' said Miles.

❖ ❖ ❖

The next day, Mrs Grose found the time to say to me quietly, 'Have you written, Miss?'

'Yes, I've written.'

The letter was in my pocket. I intended to send it later. Meanwhile, my pupils had been brilliant all morning. It was as if they were determined to ignore tensions by performing well at arithmetic and showing their brilliance at history. Miles, in particular, was a charming little gentleman. Anyone who didn't know him would think him extraordinary, but I knew he understood evil. He was also a little gentleman after lessons, when he asked if I would like him to come and play the piano for me for half an hour. It was a charming exhibition of tact[3]; he was telling me that he liked me and that he was only fighting for a principle. I was so far under his influence while he was playing that I almost thought I had been asleep. I hadn't really slept, I had

---

1. blown out: （窗子）因大風而爆裂　　　**3. tact:** 機智

2. jubilation: 歡慶

done something much worse, I had forgotten. Where was Flora? I asked Miles who simply laughed out loud, 'How should I know?' and started singing.

I went straight to my room, but his sister wasn't there, so I looked in a few other rooms. She wasn't there, so I went downstairs to the servants' hall. Mrs Grose was in the housekeeper's room, alone. I thought she might be with the maids, so we separated to look for her. No luck. I was sure she had gone out, so I voiced my fear to Mrs Grose.

'Without a hat?'

'That woman never wears one.'

'She's with *her*?'

'She's with her!' I declared. 'We must find them.'

Mrs Grose was uneasy. 'And where's Master Miles?'

'Oh, he's with Quint. They're in the schoolroom. They have played their trick,' I continued, 'He found a divine[1] way to keep me quiet.'

'Divine?' exclaimed Mrs Grose.

'Infernal[2], then,' I said, almost cheerfully, 'Come on.'

'Are you leaving Miles?'

'Yes, I don't mind that now.' I pulled the letter out of my pocket and put it on the hall table. 'Luke will take this,' I said. I walked over to the front door, opened it and stood on the step. The storm was over, but the afternoon was damp and wet. We had no hats or coats as we went off down the drive in search of Flora. ■

---

1. divine: 天賜的、極好的   **2. infernal:** 地獄的、可恨的

Reading Comprehension

1 **Answer the questions, true (T) or false (F). Correct the false answers.**

                T   F

1 The governess goes into church after Miles. ☐ ☐
_____

2 Miles doesn't want to leave Bly for school. ☐ ☐
_____

3 The governess sees Miss Jessel's ghost in the schoolroom. ☐ ☐
_____

4 Mrs Grose would prefer the governess not to write to the children's uncle. ☐ ☐
_____

5 The governess goes to speak to Miles that night. ☐ ☐
_____

6 Flora wants her uncle to come to Bly as soon as possible. ☐ ☐
_____

7 The governess tells Miles she can't save him. ☐ ☐
_____

8 Mrs Grose has written a letter to the uncle. ☐ ☐
_____

9 Flora has disappeared. ☐ ☐
_____

10 The governess sends Luke to look for Flora. ☐ ☐
_____

Writing

2 **Write the governess's letter to the children's uncle**
- apologize for contacting him
- summarize the problem
- explain what action you would like him to take

Vocabulary

3 **In Chapter Six, the governess says "I knew I had gone too far",
meaning that she had been too extreme.**

**Put the right form of these expressions using *go* into the sentences
below. Use your dictionary to help you.**

> go over the top • be on the go • have a go at (something)
> have a go at (someone) • make a go of (something)
> go off with (something)

1 I can't do my maths homework. Pete _____ my book.
2 She bought 300 cakes for a party with 150 guests. She

_____.

3 He was really tired. He had _____ all day.
4 I want the business to succeed. I really want to _____ it.
5 I think the head teacher was unfair. She really _____ me
for being late.
6 I'd like to _____ hang-gliding. It looks fun!

Vocabulary

4 Use your dictionary to help you. Which of these is the odd one out? Give your reasons.

1 a ☐ mosque   **b** ☐ temple   **c** ☐ church   **d** ☐ library

2 a ☐ strange   **b** ☐ similar   **c** ☐ odd   **d** ☐ peculiar

3 a ☐ sort out   **b** ☐ tidy   **c** ☐ organize   **d** ☐ remove

4 a ☐ shout   **b** ☐ scream   **c** ☐ cry   **d** ☐ whisper

5 a ☐ lamplight **b** ☐ candlelight **c** ☐ moonlight **d** ☐ torchlight

FCE – Grammar

5 Complete the second sentence so that it has a similar meaning to the first sentence, using the word given. **Do not change the word given.** You must use between two and five words, including the word given.

1 I was less frightened of the ghosts than I'd expected.
weren't
The ghosts .... I'd expected.

2 If you don't write the letter, the children's uncle won't know.
unless
The children's uncle .... write the letter.

3 We ought to look for Flora.
better
We .... Flora.

4 'Do not put out the candle, Flora!' said the governess.
not
The governess .... put out the candle.

5 'I won't wear my hat!' she exclaimed.
refused
She .... hat.

Vocabulary

6a **Confusing Words. What's the difference between the following words? Use your dictionary to help you and write a definition of each word.**

- shade/shadow
- carefree/careless
- cooker/cook
- lend/borrow
- a water glass/a glass of water

1 Shade	_____	Shadow		_____
2 Carefree	_____	Careless		_____
3 Cooker	_____	Cook		_____
4 Lend	_____	Borrow		_____
5 Water glass	_____	Glass of water		_____

6b **Choose the correct alternative in the sentences below.**

1 I was boiling hot, so I stood in the *shade/shadow* of an old oak tree.

2 I felt liberated. I was completely *carefree/careless*.

3 That zabaglione was perfect. He really is a very good *cooker/cook*.

4 I'm going to have to *lend/borrow* the money from the bank.

5 She poured me an ice-cold *water glass/glass of water*.

PRE-READING ACTIVITIES

Speaking

7a **Flora is missing. Where do you think she is? Tick the options and add two more ideas of your own.**

She must have gone for a walk. ☐

She might have run away from home. ☐

Miss Jessel could have come to take her away. ☐

Perhaps she's run away to stay with her uncle. ☐

_____

_____

7b **Work in pairs. Discuss your opinions about Flora's disappearance. Then read and check.**

Chapter Seven

"Sometimes, she's not a child ..."

We went straight to the lake. I knew that Flora loved to be near the water or in sit in the small boat that was kept there. When Mrs Grose realized where we were going, she showed her surprise. 'You're going to the water, Miss. Do you think she's *in* –'

'She may be. But I think she may be in the place where Miss Jessel appeared. I have always expected her to go back there. And now her brother has helped her.'

Mrs Grose stopped. 'Do you really think they *talk* about them?'

'I'm sure they say things that would horrify us.'

'And Miss Jessel is with her?'

'Yes. You'll see.'

'No, thank you!' cried my friend and she stood firmly in her place. I went on without her. By the time I reached the pool, however, she was following me again. She sighed with relief when she saw that the child was not there. Flora was not on the near side of the lake and I couldn't see her on the far side, where there were some trees. We looked at the empty expanse of the lake.

'She's taken the boat!' I cried.

'All alone? That child?'

'She's not alone and sometimes she's not a child: she's an old, old woman.' I started to walk around the edge of the lake which was quite narrow, but very long. It would take us about ten minutes to get to where I was sure we would find Flora. In some places, it was difficult to walk because there was no path, and sometimes I had to slow down to help Mrs Grose. When we reached the other side of the lake, the boat was where I had thought it would be, almost out of sight. We went through the gate in the fence. 'There she is!' we both exclaimed at once. Flora was standing, smiling, on the grass. Her performance was complete. She waited for us to go to her and smiled and smiled. Mrs Grose fell to her knees and took the child in her arms. Flora looked at me over our companion's shoulder. Her face was serious now. I envied Mrs Grose; her relationship with the child was so simple and mine was so complex. Mrs Grose got up, took the child's hand and walked over to me. Her expression was clear: I have nothing to say, the look said. Flora was the first to speak. 'Where's Miles?'

It was a brave thing to say: after weeks and weeks of silence, I was pushed to the limit. Mrs Grose stared at me, but it was too late now. I said it. 'Where, my darling, is Miss Jessel?'

Once I had said it, it was finished. We had never spoken her name before, and the shock showed on the child's face. The name was like a slap[1], the breaking of glass. Mrs Grose cried out at the same time as I gasped[2] myself. 'She's there, she's there!'

Miss Jessel stood in front of us on the opposite bank, and I now had proof. She was there and I was justified; she was there and I was neither

---

1. **slap:** 耳光　　　　　　2. **gasped:** 喘氣

cruel nor mad. She was there for poor, scared Mrs Grose, but she was there most for Flora; and I had the strangest feeling of gratitude[1] which I was sure that the pale demon would understand. She was standing straight and she was evil in person. I saw Mrs Grose was looking directly at her. Then I looked at the child. I saw how badly Flora had been affected by the creature. I was sure she would be agitated, but she didn't even look in Miss Jessel's direction, instead, she was staring at me, with a hard, serious face. It was a new expression and she seemed to read, accuse and judge me. As if to defend myself, I pointed and cried, 'She's there, *there* and you can see her as well as you can see me!'

I had said to Mrs Grose that she was like an old, old woman and this description was perfect for the moment: she simply looked more and more disapproving of me. I was more shocked by this than anything else, although I soon became aware that Mrs Grose was becoming an opponent. The next moment, my elder companion screamed out to me, 'What a terrible thing to say. I can't see anything!'

I held her arm tightly. The horrible presence was still there. It had already lasted a minute and it was still there, clear and plain for everyone to see. I pointed at her again,

'Can't you see her like *we* can see her? There, now, *there*. Look, *look!*'

She looked as I looked and denied seeing anything. She was relieved that she couldn't see anything, but I sensed that she would have supported me if she could. I felt, I saw, my predecessor win, I felt my defeat. Mrs Grose spoke to reassure the child. 'She isn't there, little lady. Nobody's there, my sweet. Miss Jessel *can't* be here, she's dead and gone. *We* know, don't we love? Let's go home as fast as we can.'

They were united in opposition to me. Flora continued to stare at me and I realized, as she stood there, holding onto our friend's dress,

1. **gratitude:** 感恩

that her childish beauty had completely vanished. She was horribly
hard; she was common and she was almost ugly.

'I don't know what you mean. I see nobody. I see nothing. I never
have. I think you're cruel!'

She hid her dreadful little face in Mrs Grose's skirt and cried, almost in
anger. 'Take me away, take me away from *her*.'

'From *me*?' I cried in horror.

'From *you*!' she screamed.

Even Mrs Grose looked at me with dismay. The horrible child had
spoken as if each of her stabbing[1] little words had come from somewhere
else. I shook my head. 'I've lost you; she is controlling you,' I pointed to
the figure across the lake. 'I've done my best, but I've lost you. Goodbye.'
I turned to Mrs Grose and shouted, 'Go! Go!'

She took the girl in her arms and ran back towards the house as fast
as she could.

I can't remember what first happened when I was left alone by the
lake. My clothes were wet, so I must have thrown myself on the ground
and cried. When I looked up, it was almost dark. I looked, through the
twilight, at the grey lake and its black, haunted edge and then I made
my long, difficult way back to the house. When I reached the gate in
the fence, I was surprised to see that the boat had gone, which made me
think again about Flora's command of the situation.

Flora spent that night with Mrs Grose, which was the best solution. I
saw neither of them when I returned, but I did spend a lot of time with
Miles. I knew that the time had come and, there was an extraordinarily
sweet sadness in the moment. When I had got back to the house, I hadn't
even looked for the boy; I had simply gone to my room to change. Flora's
possessions had all gone. I went into the schoolroom, but I asked Miles

1. **stabbing:** 像刀刺般的痛

no questions at all. He had his freedom now, he could have it forever. He used his freedom to come and sit with me at about eight o'clock in absolute silence. After tea, I had blown out the candles, conscious of a mortal coldness: I felt as if I would never be warm again. When Miles appeared, I was sitting with my thoughts. He paused by the door then came to sit in the chair opposite. We sat there, in absolute stillness, but I felt that he wanted to be with me.

◆◆◆

Very early the next morning, Mrs Grose had bad news. Flora had a fever; she had hardly slept and it was clear that she was afraid of me, not Miss Jessel. I got up. 'Does she still deny seeing Miss Jessel?'

Mrs Grose was sad, 'I don't want to push her.'

'I can imagine what she is saying. She is proud, she doesn't tell lies, she's a lady, she's respectable. She'll never speak to me again.'

Mrs Grose was silent for a moment. Then she agreed, 'You're right, she won't speak to you. She asks me every three minutes if I think you're coming in.'

'I see. Has she said anything since yesterday to show that she is in contact with Miss Jessel?'

'No. And you know,' continued my friend, 'then and there by the lake, I agree with her, there was no-one.'

'And you still think that?'

'Of course, what can I do?'

'Nothing. She's the cleverest person in the world. Their two friends have made them cleverer than nature made them. Flora will harm me. She'll tell her uncle that I'm the worst person. Flora wants to get rid of me[1].'

---

1. **to get rid of:** 趕走

'She never wants to see you again,' said my companion bravely.

'You think I should go. But I have a better idea. I think *you* should go. You must take Flora. You must take her away from here, straight to her uncle.'

'What about you?'

'I'll stay here with Miles. I want to try. Take his sister and leave him alone with me.' I was amazed at my courage. 'But there is one thing. They mustn't see each other, not even for three seconds, before she goes. They haven't seen each other, have they?'

'No, no. She's safe. But are you sure about the little gentleman?'

'I'm not sure of anything except *you*. But I think he wants to speak. Last night, he sat with me in the firelight for two hours as if something were coming.'

'Did it come?' she asked, looking through the window at the grey, early morning.

'No, he needs more time.'

My friend seemed quite reluctant[1]. 'What do you mean by more time?'

'A day or two. Then he'll be on *my* side, which is important. If he says nothing, I shall only fail and you will have helped me by doing whatever you can in London.'

I could see she was embarrassed, but she agreed. 'I'll go. I'll go this morning.'

'Are you sure?'

'I can't stay.'

She looked at me in such a way that I jumped at the possibilities. 'Since yesterday, have you seen –?'

'I've *heard*. I've heard such horrible things from the child this morning. She says such things!' She dropped onto the sofa and cried.

'Thank God!' I cried, 'It justifies me!'

---

1. reluctant: 不情願

'It does, Miss!'

I hesitated. 'Is she so very horrible?'

'Really shocking. She says such terrible things about you, Miss. I don't know where she picked up –'

'Such bad language? I do.'

My friend was even more serious. 'I must get her away from here. Far from this. Far from *them*.'

'You think she can be free. In spite of yesterday, you *believe* –'

'I believe.'

We stood shoulder to shoulder. I spoke again, 'There is one good thing. My letter will have arrived in London before you.'

Mrs Grose sounded tired. 'Your letter was never sent.'

'What happened to it?'

'I don't know. Master Miles –'

'Did he take it?' I interrupted.

'I saw, when I came back with Miss Flora that the letter wasn't where you left it. Later in the evening, I asked Luke and he said he hadn't even seen it.'

'If Miles took it, he's probably read it and destroyed it.'

'You see!' she said, almost elated, 'Now I understand what he must have done at school. He stole!'

I thought about what she was saying. 'Well, perhaps.'

'He stole *letters*!'

'If he stole my letter to his uncle, then he will be ashamed of himself. I will talk to him. He will have the chance to confess[1]. If he confesses, he can save himself. And if he's saved –'

'Then you are?'

The dear woman kissed me and left. 'I'll save you!' She cried as she left.

---

1. to confess: 承認

Reading Comprehension

1 Answer the questions about Chapter Seven.

1 The governess's attitude to Flora has changed. How does she describe Flora now?

_____

2 What does Flora do when she sees the governess and Mrs Grose?

_____

3 Can Flora or Mrs Grose see the ghost of Miss Jessel at the lake?

_____

4 What does the governess do when Mrs Grose and Flora set off back to the house?

_____

5 Who comes to join the governess in the schoolroom?

_____

6 Where did Flora spend the night?

_____

7 How is Flora the next morning?

_____

8 Where does the governess tell Mrs Grose to take Flora?

_____

9 Why does the governess want to stay at Bly with Miles?

_____

10 Was the governess's letter sent to London?

_____

11 Why does the governess think Miles was sent away from school?

_____

Characters

2 Who am I? Write the name of the character next to the description.

1 I'm quite young. I wasn't born at Bly. I think I'm a strong person. I try to do my best in all situations and I'm extremely conscientious. I've been quite confused lately.
I am _____

2 I'm quite young and have recently returned to Bly after an absence of a few weeks. I'd like to resume my studies and I think I'd rather spend more time away from Bly.
I am _____

3 I used to work at Bly. I left last year after an unhappy love affair. People used to think I was quite pretty. Some people questioned my judgement when I fell in love with a servant.
I am _____

FCE – Grammar

3 Use the word given in capitals at the end of some of the lines to form a word that fits in the gap in the same line.

Henry James was born in New York City, in 1843. He was of both Scottish and Irish **1** _____ . James went to Harvard to	**DESCEND**
study law, although he didn't really have a **2** _____ mind. He started to write	**LAW**
literary reviews and he soon gained a reputation for **3** _____ . He moved	**BRILLIANT**
to London in 1876. He wrote many plays and novels although, to his **4** _____	**DISAPPOINT**
the plays were generally **5** _____	**SUCCESS**
James eventually became known as the master of the **6** _____ novel.	**PSYCHOLOGY**

Vocabulary

4 **There are a lot of references to legal language in Chapter Seven. Match the words in the box to the definitions below.**

> accuse *v* • judge *n (+ v)* • defend *v* • evidence *n*
> admit *v* • guilty *adj* • witness *n (+ v)* • prove *v*

1 A person who has seen a crime is a _____ to that crime.

2 A person who must decide something is a _____.

3 Proof is the noun. The verb is _____.

4 Someone who has committed a crime is _____ of that crime.

5 To convict someone of a crime, the court needs _____.

6 To say that someone has done something wrong is _____ someone.

7 To say that you have done something wrong is _____ something.

8 You have the right to _____ yourself, if someone says you have committed a crime.

Writing and Speaking

5a **Work in pairs. Consider these points about Flora:**

• Is she possessed by the spirit of Miss Jessel?
• Is she tormented by a mad governess?
• Is she just a normal child?

5b **Make notes about the encounter by the lake in Chapter Seven *from Flora's point of view*. Explain:**

• Why you were by the lake
• How you felt
• What happened after

5c Use your notes to write an account of what happened.

```



```

PRE-READING ACTIVITIES

Speaking

6 Work in pairs. Discuss what you think happens in the last chapter to:
- Flora
- Mrs Grose
- the governess
- Miles
- Miss Jessel
- Peter Quint

Explain your reasons.

Listening

7a What do you think? Are these statements about Chapter Eight true or false?

		T	F
1	Flora and Mrs Grose leave the next morning.	☐	☐
2	The governess sends Miles to a new school.	☐	☐
3	Miles refuses to have lessons in the schoolroom.	☐	☐
4	Miles disappears.	☐	☐
5	The governess has dinner in the family dining room.	☐	☐
6	Miles is very worried about Flora.	☐	☐

▶ 9 **7b** Now listen to the beginning of Chapter Eight and check your answers.

Chapter Eight

"Alone with the quiet day."

Mrs Grose and Flora left for London before the morning was over. When she had gone, I missed her greatly and I began to realize what I was facing. I was alone against the elements. The maids and men could not help, they simply looked blank, and a little confused at events, so I became very grand and very dry. All I could do was to hold on to the helm to avoid a total wreck[1]. I wandered around the house, appearing firm, but I paraded[2] with a sick heart.

Miles was obviously unconcerned. I hadn't seen him at all as I walked around the house, but everyone knew that there had been a change in our relationship since he had helped Flora, by playing the piano for me, the day before. It was obvious that there had been a problem, since Flora had been kept away from him, and had now gone, and there were no lessons in the schoolroom.

He had already disappeared when I checked his room in the morning and the maids said he had had his breakfast and gone out for a walk. This showed that he understood that there was a change in my status. We had not yet decided what this change would mean. There was no reason to pretend that I had anything more to teach him. He had his freedom now and I could never touch it again; I

---

1. wreck: 船隻殘骸　　　　　**2. paraded:** 雄赳赳地走路

had shown this the night before, in the schoolroom, when I had not spoken to him. When he finally arrived, it was clear that the beautiful boy was not in the least worried by events.

To show my high status in the house, I had decided to have dinner in the dining room, with the boy. Sitting in this room, outside which I had first received information from Mrs Grose, I felt that my equilibrium depended on my iron will[1], the will to close my eyes to the fact that the truth I was facing was against nature. I had to force myself to take an unusual and demanding direction, which was, after all, just another turn of the screw of ordinary human virtue. I had no choice but to plunge into the terrible obscure. I saw again what was so rare in my little companion. Perhaps he had found another delicate way to make me feel at ease, just as he did during lessons. There was light in the way we shared our solitude. Why had he been given such intelligence? Surely his intelligence would save him. It was as if, in the dining room, he had shown me the way. The roast lamb was on the table and the servants had gone. Before he sat down, Miles stood for a moment with his hands in his pockets looking at the meat. Was he going to make a humorous comment? I wondered. No, what he said was, 'I say, my dear, is she really very awfully ill?'

'Little Flora? I'm sure she'll soon be better. London will be good for her. Bly didn't agree with her any more. Come here and get your dinner.'

He obeyed and carried the plate to his seat. When he had sat in his place, he continued, 'Was this a sudden problem with Bly?'

'No, not so sudden.'

'Why didn't you send her away before?'

'Before what?'

1. iron will: 堅定的意志

'Before she became too ill to travel.'

'She's *not* too ill to travel. She would have become too ill, if she had stayed. The journey will take away the influence.'

'I see.' Miles was being grand too.

He ate his meal with charming manners, as usual. They had expelled him from school, but clearly not for bad table manners. He was irreproachable as always, but a little more self-conscious today. He sat in silence while he thought about his situation.

Our meal was very short and I soon called the servants to clear the table. Miles stood with his hands in his little pockets and his back to me and looked out of the window through which, that day, I had seen what shocked me. We were silent while the maid was in the room – as silent as a young couple on their honeymoon who feel shy in the presence of the waiter. He turned round when the maid had left us. 'Well – so we're alone!'

'More or less.' I went pale, 'Not completely. We wouldn't like that.'

'No, I suppose we wouldn't. Of course, we have the others. But then, the others aren't very important.'

'It depends what you mean by "very"!'

'Yes, everything depends.'

He turned back to the window. He leaned his head against the glass looking at the plants and the signs of November. I had my hypocritical mending 'work', so I sat on the sofa, hiding behind it. I prepared myself for the worst. I usually did this when I knew that the children were doing something from which I was barred. Strangely, I didn't feel barred now. I began to realize that *he* was. The squares in the window were an image, a kind of failure. He felt shut in or shut out. Was he looking for something he couldn't see? It was the first time that he had felt like this and it made him anxious. He was trying to control himself, but he had been anxious all day. He had worked hard at dinner pretending to be calm and well-mannered. When he turned round he was to say, 'Well. I'm glad Bly agrees with me!'

'Well, I think you've seen a lot more of it in these twenty-four hours than you have before. I hope you've enjoyed it.'

'Oh, yes. I've been a long way today. Miles and miles away. I've never been so free.'

'Well, do you like it?'

He stood there, smiling. 'Do *you?*' he asked. Before I could answer, he continued, 'You're taking it very well. If we're alone together at the moment, you are more alone than I am. But I hope you don't mind.'

'I don't mind spending time with you, dear child. I enjoy it greatly, although you are free not to spend time with me. Why else would I stay?'

He looked at me directly and his face was the most beautiful I had ever seen. 'Do you stay just for *that?*'

'Of course, I am your friend and take an interest in you. I want to help you. Don't you remember the night of the storm when I said that there was nothing in the world I wouldn't do for you?'

'Yes! Yes! But I think that was because you wanted me to do something for *you.*'

'Partly. But you didn't.'

'Yes. You wanted me to tell you something,' he said with superficial brightness, 'That's why you've stayed.'

He seemed happy, but there was perhaps some resentment[1]. This was a suggestion of surrender. He waited a long time. 'Do you want me to say now. Here?'

---

1. **resentment:** 怨恨

'It's the right time and the right place.'

He looked around him and I thought for a moment that he was afraid. I heard myself speak to him gently. 'Do you want to go out again like today?'

'Yes,' He smiled heroically although he was in pain. He had picked up his hat and was playing with it. I was aware of the horror of what I was doing. It was an act of violence. I was pushing the idea of horror and guilt on a small helpless creature. We circled around each other like fighters who were keeping their distance. That kept us safe for a while. 'I'll tell you everything,' said Miles, 'I'll tell you anything you like and you'll stay here with me and we'll both be alright. I will tell you, but not now.'

'Why not now?'

He turned away from me and stood at the window in total silence. Then he turned with the air of someone who had to meet someone outside. 'I have to see Luke.'

This was the first time I had made him tell a vulgar lie and I was ashamed. His lies made my truth. 'Go to Luke and I'll wait. Just answer one unimportant question.'

'Yes.'

'Tell me,' I stared down at my work, 'Did you, yesterday afternoon, from the table in the hall, take my letter?'

❖ ❖ ❖

Before I could assess his reaction, a sudden feeling made me jump up and hold him close to me, keeping his back to the window. I had sensed that Peter Quint was at the window. He was in full view, like a guard standing in front of a prison. I saw that he had reached the window and that he was close to the glass, staring though it. He offered the room his white face of damnation[1]. At that moment, I made my decision. I had to stop the boy from seeing the presence, even though I could see it. It was like fighting with a demon for a human soul. The face close to mine was as close as the face against the glass. Finally, he spoke.

'Yes, I took it.'

I was filled with joy and held him close. I could feel the little fever in his tiny body and the strong beat of his heart. I kept my eyes on the thing at the window and saw it move. Now it was like a wild animal. It was watching and waiting. 'What did you take it for?'

'To see what you said about me.'

'You opened the letter?'

'I opened it.'

I now held him a little distant. Miles was uneasy. His communication had stopped. He knew he was in a presence, but not of what. My eyes went back to the window and I saw that the air was clear. I had triumphed and there was nothing there. 'And you found nothing.'

He shook his head[2].

'Nothing.'

'So what have you done with it?' I kissed his forehead.

'I burnt it.'

'Is that what you did at school?'

'At school?'

'Did you take things?'

'Did I *steal*?'

I reddened. 'Was this why you can't go back?'

He was surprised. 'Did you know?'

---

1. damnation: 責難   2. shook his head: 搖頭

'I know everything.'

'I didn't steal.'

I shook him tenderly. 'What did you do then?'

He looked, in pain, all around the room. It was difficult for him to breathe. He might have been at the bottom of the sea, looking for some green twilight.

'I said things.'

'Only that?'

'I suppose I shouldn't have said them.'

'To whom?'

He tried to remember, but couldn't. 'I don't know!' he said.

He almost smiled as he surrendered. I should have left it there, but I was blind with victory. 'Was it to everyone?' I asked.

'No, it was only to –', he shook his head, 'I don't remember their names.'

'Were there many of them?'

'No, only the ones I liked.'

I seemed to float into obscurity[1] not light. Within a minute I wondered if he were innocent. If he were innocent, what, then, was I? I was paralyzed[2] and let him go a little and he moved a little towards the clear window. I now felt that I had nothing to keep him from. 'And did they repeat what you said?'

He was soon away from me, still breathing hard. He was no longer angry with me for holding on to him. As he had done before, he looked outside at the dark day. 'Oh yes, they must have repeated it. To those *they* liked,' he added.

'And the teachers found out?'

'Yes. But I didn't know they'd tell.'

---

1. **obscurity:** 朦朧   2. **paralyzed:** 癱瘓、動彈不得

'The masters? They didn't. They've never told. That's why I'm asking you.'

He turned his beautiful, fevered face to me. 'Yes, it was too bad to write home.'

It was such a contradiction coming from such a speaker. 'Nonsense!' I said forcefully, 'What were these things?'

I was angry at his judge, his executioner, but he turned away. I had to jump to hold him in my arms again, because the white face of damnation had appeared again against the glass to stop his confession. I felt sick at the end of my victory and the return of the battle. 'No more, no more, no more!' I screamed as I pressed him against me.

'Is she *here*?' Miles panted as he saw where I was looking. The 'she' terrified me and I echoed it, 'Miss Jessel, Miss Jessel!' He cried with a sudden fury.

I was horrified. 'It's not Miss Jessel! But it's there, in front of us, the coward horror, there for the last time!'

He gave a frantic movement and, shaking for air and light, he was at me, in a white rage, staring all over the place, unable to see. 'It's *he*?'

'Who do you mean?'

'Peter Quint – you devil!' He looked around the room again, 'Where?'

They are in my ears still. The surrender of the name and his tribute to my devotion. 'It doesn't matter now! *I* have you! He has lost you for ever! There, *there*!' I said to Miles.

He had already looked round, stared and seen, seen only the quiet day. He cried with the loss I was so proud of and fell into the abyss[1]. I caught him, yes. I held him, you can imagine with what passion; but at the end of a minute I began to feel what I really held.

---

1. **abyss:** 深淵

We were alone, with the quiet day, and his little heart, dispossessed[1], had stopped.

1. **dispossessed:** 被剝奪

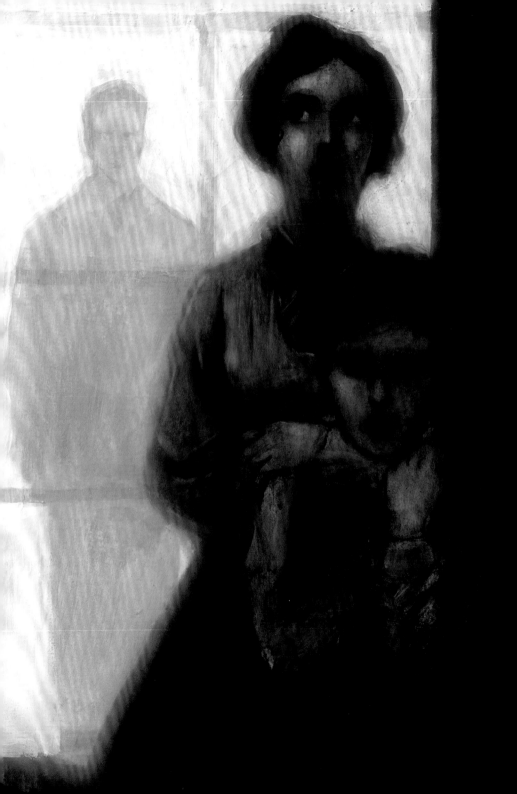

Reading Comprehension

1 **Answer the questions about Chapter Eight. Support your answers with evidence from the text.**

1 How does the governess describe her feelings after Mrs Grose and Flora have left for London?

_____
_____

2 How does the governess think Miles is feeling?

_____
_____

3 Why, in your opinion, does the governess feel it necessary to show her "high status"?

_____
_____

4 The governess tells Miles why she has decided to stay with him. What explanation does she give?

_____
_____

5 Why did Miles take the letter?

_____
_____

6 According to Miles, why was he expelled?

_____
_____

7 Who sees the ghost of Peter Quint at the window? Miles, the governess, or both of them?

_____
_____

8 What were Miles's last words before he died?

_____
_____

Speaking

2 **Work in pairs. Discuss your answers and give reasons for them.**

- Are the ghosts real or are they in the governess's imagination?
- Are the children innocent or are they under the ghosts' influence?
- Did your opinion of the governess and the children change at different points in the story?
- When Miles says '– you Devil!' is he referring to Quint or the governess?
- Did you enjoy reading *The Turn of the Screw?*

FCE – Writing

3 **You recently saw this notice in an English-language magazine called Literature Today.**

REVIEWS NEEDED!

Have you read any books recently? If so, we want your review. All you need to do is give an overview of the plot, the characters and the setting and say whether you would recommend the book to other people.

The best reviews will appear on the magazine website.

Write your review in 120–180 words.

Henry James (1843 - 1916)

Henry James was an American writer who spent much of his life in England. He was one of the major novelists of the late 19th and early 20th centuries, writing a total of 20 novels. He also wrote plays, more than 100 short stories, as well as essays, works of literary criticism and an autobiography.

Early Life

He was born on April 15th, 1843 in New York City and was the second of five children. His father, Henry James (Senior), was a well-known theological writer and intellectual, and the family mixed socially with some of the greatest writers and thinkers of the time. Henry James Senior felt that a wide education was very important and, in 1855, when young Henry was only 12 years old, the family set off on a 3-year tour of Europe. Henry was tutored in the language and literature of the countries that the family visited. His international education made him a great reader of literature from many different countries and influenced his writing.

Writing Career

When Henry was 19 years old, he went to Harvard to study law. However, he only stayed a year, realizing that he much preferred reading literature to the law. This was the start of his writing career and, in 1864, he published his first story in a monthly magazine.

In 1869 Henry left America for Europe. He lived in Italy and then in Paris, where he wrote his first novel, *Watch and Ward*. He moved to London in 1876, and worked as a journalist, also earning a small income from his stories and plays.

In 1879, his short novel, *Daisy Miller*, was published. It was his first great success and he went on to produce his first series of novels. Then, in 1890, he began to concentrate on writing for the theatre. Unfortunately, in 1895, his play, *Guy Domville*, was a total disaster and Henry stopped writing plays. Soon after this, he moved away from London and went to live in a large house in the south of England. This was where, in 1898, he wrote *The Two Magics*, a collection of stories which included *The Turn of the Screw*.

Later Years

In 1904, Henry returned to America for the first time in twenty years. He gave a series of lectures in many different locations, before returning to England. Over the next few years, he visited America more frequently than before, although he remained resident in England for the rest of his life. In 1915 he became a British Citizen in protest at America's refusal to enter the First World War. He was also awarded the Order of Merit. Later that year, he suffered a stroke. He died in February 1916.

The Three Periods

Henry James's novels are often divided into three periods of James's life.

THE FIRST PERIOD
MAINLY ANGLO-AMERICAN SUBJECTS
Daisy Miller, Washington Square, Portrait of a Lady and *The Bostonians.*

THE SECOND PERIOD
PURELY ENGLISH SUBJECTS
The Tragic Muse, The Spoils of Poynton, What Maisie Knew and *The Awkward age.*

THE LAST PERIOD
ANGLO-AMERICAN
The Wings of a Dove, The Ambassadors and *The Golden Bowl.*

Daisy Miller first edition (1878)

Task
Complete the form with the information about Henry James.

Name: _____
Date of birth: _____
Occupation: _____
Place of birth: _____
Number of novels written: _____
First novel: _____
Date of *The Turn of the Screw*: _____
Reason he became a British citizen: _____
Date of death: _____

Themes and Symbols

Innocence and Evil

In *The Turn of the Screw*, one of the most obvious themes is the corruption of innocence. If we think the governess is trying to save the children, then Miss Jessel and Peter Quint are trying to corrupt them. If we think the ghosts are in the governess's imagination, then she is corrupting them. We never find out what form the corruption takes, this is deliberately left to the reader's imagination. Likewise, we never find out why Miles has been expelled from school, or how Miss Jessel died, but the suggestion of evil is there.

Portrait of Denis Mackail, grandson of the artist by Sir Edward Burne-Jones.

Beauty

Beauty is another important theme, as it is often used as a contrast to evil. When the governess first meets Flora, she is struck by her beauty and this is associated with her goodness. Later in the story, however, the governess comes to feel that Flora is evil and she describes the child as "almost ugly". When Mrs Grose and the governess talk about Miles's expulsion from school, they give his beauty as a reason for him being incapable of bad behaviour. Miss Jessel is described as "wonderfully beautiful", and this is contrasted with her behaviour, which Mrs Grose calls "infamous". Bly itself is described as beautiful and like a fairytale castle, at the same time as being "ugly". In the prologue, Douglas describes the governess's handwriting as beautiful, even though the story itself is clearly not.

Heroism

The governess sees herself as heroic in trying to save the children from Quint and Jessel. She could ask for help from the children's uncle, but knows he doesn't want to be involved. She doesn't even involve him after receiving the letter from Miles's school. The governess regards her own courage as "magnificent", as she faces the ghosts alone and tries to protect the children from them. Even at the end, when Flora is ill, she sends Mrs Grose away with her and stays to continue her fight for Miles against the ghosts. The death of Miles shows that her heroism was misplaced and destructive.

Light

Light is used as a symbol throughout the novel. Twilight is often associated with the ghosts; the governess first sees Peter Quint at twilight and the lake is described as "haunted" at twilight. Candlelight is an important protection for the governess.

When her candle goes out on the stairs, the governess meets the ghost of Quint. Likewise, her candle is blown out twice more in important scenes, once when she suspects that Flora has blown it out and again when she is talking to Miles about school.

Silence

The sound of birds cawing around Bly is an important symbol, especially as it stops at key moments. When the governess meets the ghosts, she refers to "intense silence".

For example, when she meets Quint on the stairs, she talks about hearing the silence and the "dead silence". In the final chapter, when the governess is battling with Miles, silence plays its part.

Task

Look back at the text find other examples where Henry James uses.

- Light
- Innocence
- Evil
- Silence
- Beauty

Interpretations

The Turn of the Screw has always presented a series of problems to critics. Traditionally, they have divided into two camps: Apparitionists and Hallucinationists. Apparitionists generally believe that the governess really sees the ghosts and is a rational narrator who simply tells us what she sees. Hallucinationists take the view that the ghosts are in her imagination and that she is an unreliable narrator. They feel she is neurotic and possibly insane. Many more modern interpretations suggest that the novella is brilliant because we never know for certain whether the ghosts are real or not.

Apparitionists

According to Apparitionists, there is a lot of evidence in the text to show that the governess is reliable as a person and a narrator. In the Prologue, Douglas calls the governess "extremely clever and nice", suggesting that she is a good, kind person. In addition, when she first meets the children, the governess is very positive about them. In the Apparitionist view, the governess is absolutely heroic as she battles against evil, trying to save the children.

Hallucinationists

According to Hallucinationists, however, there is a lot of evidence in the text to show that the governess is unreliable. They say that the whole story of events at Bly is told by the governess and narrated from her point of view. We never know whether anyone else sees the ghosts. Her relationship towards the children is seen as very volatile. Hallucinationists tend to argue that the governess is overprotective of the children and repressed. Her madness, therefore, is the reason for the destruction of the children.

Ambiguity

Many critics still take the view that the book is a masterpiece *because* it is ambiguous. They argue that we never know for sure whether the governess sees the ghosts, or whether she imagines them. Henry James often makes us change our minds as we read the novella: one minute we are sure that the governess is really fighting against evil, the next minute we think the ghosts are only in her imagination.

Henry James's view

What did the author himself say about the novella? Henry James wrote many letters to his readers, other writers and critics. However, James was enigmatic. Sometimes he said that he was only interested in writing a traditional ghost story. On other occasions he stated his aim of writing a 'fairy story' to lead readers towards horror created by their own imaginations. When talking about the governess's character, once he called her "courageous", yet, in a different letter, he talked about the "false friends" of the children. James was even ambiguous about whether he regarded *The Turn of the Screw* as a good piece of writing, or not – in one journal he called it "inferior" as a novella, but then analyzed it more positively elsewhere.

Task

What do you think?

Is the governess is a reliable or unreliable narrator? Why?

Is she a guardian of the children or an overprotective adult?

Is *The Turn of the Screw* a traditional ghost story or a psychological thriller?

Adaptations

Over the years there have been many adaptations of the story of *The Turn of the Screw*, on film, on television and in music.

On film

One of the most highly regarded film adaptations of *The Turn of the Screw* is a film by Jack Clayton called *The Innocents* (1961). The cast includes Michael Redgrave and Megs Jenkins, with Deborah Kerr as the neurotic governess. It was one of the last black and white supernatural horror films to be made in Britain and, in it, Deborah Kerr gives probably the finest screen performance of her career. Jack Clayton's direction gives the film a very tense and haunting atmosphere and echoes the themes of Henry James's novel. Also, just like Henry James's novel, the film doesn't tell us whether the ghosts are real, or a product of the governess's imagination. One of the critics described the film as "The best ghost movie I've ever seen."

Other film versions of note are:
The Others (2001) starring Nicole Kidman. This is not an actual adaptation, but is partly based on the novel and was heavily influenced by *The Innocents*.

In a Dark Place (2006) starring Leelee Sobieski (*Eyes Wide Shut*) is based upon the novel.

On television

In recent years, the BBC have produced two television adaptations of *The Turn of the Screw*.

The first was in 1999, starring Jodhi May as the governess and Pam Ferris as Mrs Grose. Colin Firth (*Pride and Prejudice*) also makes an appearance as the uncle. This version keeps very close to the original Henry James novel and much of the dialogue comes directly from the book. A lot of the reviews say that it is one of the best television adaptations, precisely because it maintains all of Henry James's themes and ideas. It uses a lot of psychological imagery to create atmosphere, rather than going for special effects. Fans of Henry James liked it a lot.

In 2009, the BBC produced another television version of *The Turn of the Screw* starring Michelle Dockery as Ann, the governess, and Sue Johnston as Mrs Grose. The film also introduced two young actors, Eva Sayer as Flora and Josef Lindsay as Miles. This adaptation was set in the 1920s and doesn't leave as much to the imagination as previous versions. The children definitely come across as spooky and the ghosts are definitely real, very unlike Henry James's story. Reviews of this version were generally good, despite the fact that some critics thought it was too different from the original novel.

In music

In 1954, Benjamin Britten wrote an opera based on *The Turn of the Screw*. It was commissioned for the Venice Biennio and was first performed at the Fenice theatre, Venice, in September of that year. The cast included Jennifer Vyvyan as the governess, Peter Pears as Quint and David Hemmings as Miles. Benjamin Britten conducted the first performance himself and the opera received outstanding reviews, with one critic even saying, "It is the best contribution England has made to a largely Italian art-form". There have been a lot of other recordings of the opera since Britten's own version, but most reviewers still believe the original 1954 version is the best.

Task

Internet research. Choose one of the following:

a) Find out more about film versions of *The Turn of the Screw* and write a paragraph like one of the ones above.

b) There have been several adaptations of *The Turn of the Screw* specially written for the theatre. Choose one and write a paragraph like one of the ones above.

TEST YOURSELF 自測

1 Answer the questions about *The Turn of the Screw.*

1 Who reads the governess's story and who does he read it to?

2 The story is set in Bly. What do we know about Bly?

3 What is the uncle's main condition for employing a governess?

4 What is the governess's first impression of Flora?

5 Where does the governess first see a ghost?

6 What reason does Miles give for going into the garden at night?

7 Who were Peter Quint and Miss Jessel?

8 After what event does Flora become ill?

9 In the final scene, what happens to Miles?

2 Find a word in English for these definitions. The words are all from the glossary.

1 The times in the year when children are at school

2 To walk around without any special destination in mind

3 Evening, before the sky is completely dark

4 To invent a story

5 To make someone or something go away

6 To say no by turning your head left and right

SYLLABUS 語法重點和學習主題

Verbs:

Tenses with *This is the first...*,
Present Perfect Continuous,
Past Perfect Continuous,
perfect infinitives,
Future Perfect,
a wide variety of phrasal verbs,
complex passive forms,
wish/if only

Types of Clause:

Type-three conditionals.

Answer Key 答案

//

The Turn Of The Screw

Pages 6 and 7

1a

Box A	Box B
governess	looked after and taught children
gardener	was responsible for the parks and grounds
housekeeper	was responsible for running the house
butler	was in charge of the other servants
housemaid	did the cleaning and helped in the kitchen
lady's maid	looked after the mistress and her clothes
valet	looked after the master and his clothes
groom	looked after the horses and stables
cook	made the meals for the family and the servants

1b Personal answers.

2a Personal answers.

2b

noun(s)	verb	adjective(s)
death	die	deathly/dead
possession	possess	possessive
disappearance	disappear	*not applicable*
cruelty	*not applicable*	cruel
murder	murder	murdering/murderous
love	love	lovely/lovable
sickness	*not applicable*	sick

3
1 exclaim   'Oh no!' <u>exclaimed</u> Miles.
2 cry   'Help!' <u>cried</u> Flora.
3 ask   'Why are you here?' she <u>asked</u>.
4 whisper   'Shh!' he <u>whispered</u>.
5 reply   'I don't know,' <u>replied</u> the governess.
6 demand   'Tell me now,' she <u>demanded</u>.
7 continue   'And another thing,' he <u>continued</u>.
8 answer   'At ten,' they <u>answered</u>.
9 .scream   'There!' Flora <u>screamed</u>.
10 enquire   'When?' he <u>enquired</u>.

4 Personal answers.

Pages 16 to 19

1   **1** A   **2** A   **3** B   **4** A   **5** C   **6** D

2   **1** True **2** False (*Her father is poor*) **3** True **4** True **5** False (*Their parents are dead*)
6 True **7** False (*The main condition of employment is that she should never bother him and should leave him in peace*) **8** True

3a **The governess:** shy, nice, clever, young, unmarried, anxious, beautiful.
The children's uncle: fashionable, nice, bold, unmarried, pleasant, handsome, charming, fine, impressive.

3b Personal answers.

4a dreadfulness/dreadful, scariness/scary, ugliness/ugly, beauty/beautiful, shyness/shy, respectability/respectable, disappointment/disappointed, pain/painful.

4b 1 "Nothing at all that I know touches it [...] for <u>dreadful</u> – dreadfulness! [...]
For general <u>ugliness</u> and horror and pain."
2 "Yes, but that's the <u>beauty</u> of her passion."
3 "Everyone groaned in <u>disappointment</u>, so he explained."
4 "There were also a cook, a couple of maids, an old pony, an old groom and an old gardener, who were all very <u>respectable</u> indeed."

5 Personal answers.

6 *Hudson,*
I'm sure **(1)** <u>that</u> *everything is going very* **(2)** <u>well</u> *at the house in London,* **(3)** <u>as</u> *usual.*
I need you to do a couple of things for me.
First of all, I need a document from my study. You will find the document **(4)** <u>in</u> *the top drawer of my desk. The drawer is locked,* **(5)** <u>but</u> *I have enclosed the key. Make sure that you lock the drawer again, then send the document and the key back to me,* **(6)** <u>at</u> *this address. Please wrap the parcel well,* **(7)** <u>because/as</u> *the document is quite old and is important to me.*
Secondly, please forward **(8)** <u>any</u> *messages for me in the same parcel.*
Many thanks

7a Personal answers.

7b 1 False **2** False **3** False **4** True **5** True **6** True **7** False

Pages 28 to 31

1 **1** True **2** True **3** False (*She says the governess will be carried away by him.*) **4** True **5** True
6 False (*She says it's a big ugly antique of a house.*) **7** True **8** False (*She can't read.*) **9** False
(*There are no details in the letter.*) **10** False (*She died at her own home.*)

2 Personal answers.

3 **a** roomful of <u>people</u>
b pocketful of <u>coins</u>
c bagful of <u>shopping</u>
d glassful of <u>water</u>
e vaseful of <u>flowers</u>
f boxful of <u>paper</u>

4 **1** 'It's like <u>saying</u> that the little lady is harmful,' said Mrs Grose. **2** Flora seemed <u>to like</u> the governess. **3** Mrs Grose avoided <u>talking</u> to the governess. **4** Mrs Grose was very glad <u>to see</u> the governess. **5** The children's uncle sent the letter to the governess instead of <u>reading</u> it himself. **6** The governess felt lucky to be able <u>to teach</u> Flora. **7** The governess persuaded Mrs Grose <u>to listen</u> to her. **8** The governess told Flora <u>to do</u> some exercises. **9** The governess was looking forward to <u>meeting</u> Flora. **10** The governess wasn't used to <u>living</u> in such a big house.

T	O	L	I	K	E	O	O	D	E
A	O	I	T	O	T	E	A	C	H
L	I	V	H	A	O	O	O	R	J
K	S	I	T	O	L	A	S	F	X
I	O	N	O	R	I	S	S	E	F
N	I	G	D	M	S	G	A	V	E
G	O	B	O	K	T	F	Y	L	L
M	R	E	M	E	E	T	I	N	G
R	E	A	D	I	N	G	N	R	Y
S	N	U	N	D	L	R	G	C	K

5a To be or not to be, that is the question - William Shakespeare
Romeo, Romeo, wherefore art thou Romeo - William Shakespeare
I wandered lonely as a cloud - William Wordsworth
O captain! my captain! - Walt Whitman
Tyger, Tyger burning bright - Willaim Blake
It is a truth universally acknowledged that a single man in possession of a good fortune, must be in want of a wife. - Jane Austen

5b Personal answers.

6a • fresh   **B**
    • fragrant   **P**
    • innocent   **B**
    • loving   **P**
    • cunning   **B**
    • mean   **N**
    • pure   **P**
    • handsome   **P**
    • charming   **B**
    • ugly   **N**

6b Personal answers.

Pages 40 to 43

1 6-9-3-5-2-1-8-4-7

2 a) negatively surprised - horrified
b) sent away from - expelled
c) immediately - instantly
d) innocence - purity
e) extremely - incredibly
f) apart from - except (for)
g) confidential - private
h) horribly ugly - grotesque
i) fascination - charm
j) reply - add

3 **1** It <u>was the first time</u> she had ever seen a ghost. **2** If she hadn't looked up <u>she would never have seen</u> the ghost. **3** 'If <u>I were you I would/I'd</u> write to the children's uncle,' she said. **4** 'I'll <u>stand by</u> you,' she said. **5** If <u>only I hadn't seen</u> the ghost.

4 **1** as white as a <u>sheet</u> **2** as strong as an <u>ox</u> **3** as fit as a <u>fiddle</u> **4** as sick as a <u>parrot</u>
5 as light as a <u>feather</u> **6** as cool as a <u>cucumber</u>

5a

A	B
'I'll **stand by** you,' she said.	support
We'll **sort** the problem **out** ourselves.	solve
We **talked over** the problem for some hours.	discuss
My task was to **bring** these children **up**.	raise/educate
That child should be **locked up**.	put in jail
I had to **face up to** the problem.	accept and solve

5b Personal answers.

6 Personal answers.

7 Personal answers.

8a Name: Peter Quint
Hair colour and style: red, curly
Height: tall
Clothing: smart, no hat
Occupation: valet / servant
Other information: long face, beard, stands straight, dark eyebrows and sharp eyes, handsome, active, not a gentleman, wearing his master's clothes. He's dead.

Pages 52 to 55

1 **1** A **2** C **3** A **4** C **5** D **6** A

2 Personal answers.

3 Essex - the location of Bly
Essex is a county in the southeast of England. The main **1 ADMINISTRATIVE** headquarters are in the town of Chelmsford. The countryside is quite flat and marshy, especially in **2 COASTAL** areas. Stansted airport is **3 LOCATED** in Essex.
Some **4 INTERESTING** seaside resorts include Clacton and Southend. Important industries are **5 ENGINEERING** and food **6 PROCESSING**.

4 **1** beautiful **2** smart **3** kind **4** scared **5** innocent **6** icy **7** heroic **8** infamous **9** aware **10** pale

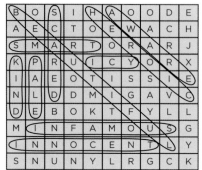

5a **1** "I don't know this man." She said <u>she didn't know that/this man.</u>
  2 "He is handsome." She said <u>he was handsome.</u>
  3 "They were both here last year." She remembered <u>that they had both been/were both here last year.</u>
  4 "The master left Quint in charge." She said <u>the master had left/left Quint in charge.</u>

5b **1** "Did Flora tell you this?" She asked whether <u>Flora had told me this.</u>
  2 "How do you know?" She asked <u>how I knew.</u>
  3 "How can you be sure? She asked <u>how I could be sure.</u>

6 Personal answers.

Pages 64 to 67

1 **1** C **2** D **3** B **4** C **5** C **6** B **7** B **8** C **9** C **10** C **11** A **12** B

2 **1** stink: it's negative, the others are positive
  2 groom: the rest are all teachers
  3 dawn: the rest are in the evening, dawn is in the morning
  4 warm: the rest are all cold
  5 gloomy: gloomy is dark, the others are light

3a **1** The governess was very proud <u>of</u> not contacting the children's uncle.
  2 Mrs Grose was ready <u>to</u> believe the governess.
  3 Miles was very good <u>at</u> playing the piano.
  4 The governess was suspicious <u>of</u> the children's behaviour.
  5 She was responsible <u>for</u> looking after the children.
  6 The children were keen <u>on</u> acting.

3b Personal answers.

4 Personal answers.

5 1A   **2**C   **3**C   **4**B   **5**D   **6**A   **7**D   **8**D

6 **1** Mrs Grose had spoken to Miles <u>despite/in spite of</u> Miss Jessel's anger.
    2 The governess walks towards the ghost <u>although/even though</u> she is afraid.
    3 The governess doesn't go to church <u>in case</u> the ghost comes for Miles.
    4 The governess describes the ghost <u>so/in case</u> Mrs Grose recognizes him.
    5 The governess accepted the job at Bly <u>despite/in spite of</u> her doubts.
    6 Mrs Grose defends Miles <u>although/even though</u> he has been expelled.

7a 2, 5, 7, 8

7b Personal answers.

Pages 76 to 79

1 **1** <u>He wanted the governess to think he was bad.</u>

    2 <u>The ghosts (Quint and Miss Jessel).</u>

    3 <u>She is afraid that Mrs Grose will disturb the children's uncle.</u>

    4 <u>Autumn.</u>

    5 <u>He asks when he can go back to school.</u>

    6 <u>That she doesn't think his uncle cares very much.</u>

2 Personal answers.

3a **Box A**

He ought to be here!
He must come here!
He needn't come here!
He has to come here!
He doesn't need to come here!
He mustn't come here!

Box B

It's his duty
There is no alternative
It is not necessary
There is no alternative
It is not necessary
There is no alternative

3b **1** Mrs Grose thinks the governess <u>ought to</u> to write to the uncle.
    2 She also thinks the uncle <u>must</u> take the children away.
    3 The governess tells Mrs Grose she <u>mustn't</u> tell the uncle.
    4 The children think they <u>ought to</u> write to their uncle
    5 Miles says his uncle <u>has to</u> come to Bly.

4 **1** The governess <u>makes/made</u> Mrs Grose keep quiet.
  2 The governess won't <u>let</u> the children talk about the past.
  3 Miles <u>makes/made</u> the governess listen to him.
  4 The governess <u>lets/let</u> Miles go into church alone.
  5 The governess doesn't <u>make</u> the children study hard.
  6 The children <u>make/made</u> the governess talk about her past.
  7 Mrs Grose <u>lets/let</u> the governess make all the important decisions.

5a-5b Personal answers.

6 **1** The governess was not <u>looking forward to</u> her next encounter with the ghosts.
  2 Miles did not want to <u>put up with</u> being educated at home for much longer.
  3 The governess is <u>looking back on</u> her past experiences as a governess at Bly.
  4 Miles <u>stood up for/stands up for</u> himself by arguing with the governess.

7 **1** False **2** True **3** True **4** False **5** True **6** False **7** False **8** True

Pages 88 to 91

1 **1** False (*She decides not to follow him into church*) **2** False (*He asks when he can go back to school*) **3** True **4** False (*She is very happy that the governess is going to write*) **5** True **6** False (*Miles wants his uncle to come to Bly*) **7** False (*She asks him to help her to save him*) **8** False (*The governess has written the letter – Mrs Grose can't read or write*) **9** True **10** False (*The governess and Mrs Grose go to look for Flora*)

2 Personal answers.

3 **1** I can't do my maths homework. Pete <u>has gone off with</u> my book.
  2 She bought 300 cakes for a party with 150 guests. She <u>went over the top.</u>
  3 He was really tired. He had <u>been on the go</u> all day.
  4 I want the business to succeed. I really want to <u>make a go of</u> it.
  5 I think the head teacher was unfair. She really <u>had a go at</u> me for being late.
  6 I'd like to <u>have a go at</u> hang-gliding. It looks fun!

4 **1** library: it's not a place of worship   **2** similar: it means the opposite of all the others
  3 remove: it means 'take away'   **4** whisper: all the other ways of speaking use noise
  5 moonlight: it's the only form of natural light

5 **1** The ghosts <u>weren't as frightening as</u> I'd expected.
  2 The children's uncle <u>won't know unless you</u> write the letter.
  3 We <u>had/'d better look for</u> Flora.
  4 The governess <u>told Flora not to</u> put out the candle.
  5 She <u>refused to wear her</u> hat.

6a **shade:** if you are in the shade you aren't in the sun. There isn't any shade at night.
shadow: your shadow is the shape you see on the ground when there is a light behind you – you can make a shadow at night

carefree: without any worries or problems
careless: not careful

cooker: a machine for cooking
cook: a person who cooks

lend: give something to someone for a temporary period – the bank often lends money to people
borrow: take something from someone for a temporary period – when people want to buy a house they often borrow money from the bank

a water glass: a glass used for water
a glass of water: a glass with water in it

6b **1** I was boiling hot, so I stood in the *shade* of an old oak tree.
2 I felt liberated. I was completely *carefree*.
3 That zabaglione was perfect. He really is a very good *cook*.
4 I'm going to have to *borrow* the money from the bank.
5 She poured me an ice-cold *glass of water*.

7a-7b Personal answers.

Pages 100 to 103

1 **1** She says Flora is sometimes not a child but an old, old woman.**2** She waits for them to go to her and she smiles and smiles.**3** No/They say they can't.**4** She throws herself on the ground and cries. **5** Miles.**6** With Mrs Grose. **7** She's ill (she has a fever). **8** To her uncle/To London. **9** She wants to try to get his trust so he will tell her about school. **10** No – Luke went to look for it but it wasn't there – Miles took it. **11** For stealing.

2 **1** I am the governess **2** I am Miles **3** I am Miss Jessel

3 **1 DESCENT** **2 LEGAL** **3 BRILLIANCE** **4 DISAPPOINTMENT**
5 UNSUCCESSFUL **6 PSYCHOLOGICAL**

4 **1** A person who has seen a crime is a witness to that crime. **2** A person who must decide something is a judge. **3** Proof is the noun. The verb is prove. **4** Someone who has committed a crime is guilty of that crime. **5** To convict someone of a crime, the court needs evidence. **6** To say that someone has done something wrong is to accuse/accusing someone. **7** To say that you have done something wrong is to admit/admitting something. **8** You have the right to defend yourself, if someone says you have committed a crime.

5a-5c Personal answers.

6 Personal answers.

7a Personal answers.

7b 1 False (*They leave the same morning*) 2 False 3 False (*There weren't any more lessons*) 4 True 5 True 6 False (*He's not in the least worried by events*)

Pages 114 to 115

1 1 The maids and men could not help, they simply looked blank a little confused at events, so I became very grand and very dry. All I could do was to hold on to the helm to avoid a total wreck. I wandered around the house, appearing firm, but I paraded with a sick heart. 2 Miles was obviously unconcerned. 3 Various answers are possible. 4 'I don't mind spending time with you, dear child. I enjoy it greatly, although you are free not to spend time with me. Why else would I stay?' 5 He wanted to see what the governess said about him. 6 Because he 'said things' to people he shouldn't have 'said things' to. 7 The governess. 8 'Peter Quint – you devil!' He looked around the room again. '*Where?*'

2 Personal answers.

3 Personal answers.

Page 117

Name: Henry James
Date of birth: 15th April 1843
Occupation: Writer
Place of birth: New York City
Number of novels written: 20
First novel: Watch and Ward
Date of *The Turn of the Screw*: 1898
Reason he became a British citizen: to protest at America's refusal to enter World War One.
Date of death: February 1916

Page 120-123

Personal answers

Page 124

1 1 Douglas – to friends at a country house. 2 It's a large country house in the south of England. It's got a large garden. Part of the house is old and part of it is modern. 3 That she won't bother him about the children. 4 That she's beautiful and angelic. 5 At the top of the tall tower. 6 He wants to show the governess he can be bad. 7 Quint was the master's valet (servant). Miss Jessel was the former governess. 8 When the governess asks her about seeing Miss Jessel's ghost at the lake. 9 He dies.

2 1 The times in the year when children are at school - <u>term time</u>
2 To walk around without any special destination in mind - <u>to wander</u>
3 Evening, before the sky is completely dark - <u>twilight</u>
4 To invent a story - <u>to make something up</u>
5 To make someone or something go away - <u>to get rid of</u>
6 To say no by turning your head left and right - <u>to shake one's head</u>

Read for Pleasure: *The Turn Of The Screw* 古堡驚魂

作　　者：Henry James

改　　寫：Janet Borsbey and Ruth Swan

繪　　畫：Rodolfo Brocchini

照　　片：Shutterstock, Getty Images

責任編輯：傅薇

封面設計：涂慧

出　　版：商務印書館（香港）有限公司
　　　　　香港筲箕灣耀興道3號東滙廣場8樓
　　　　　http://www.commercialpress.com.hk

發　　行：香港聯合書刊物流有限公司
　　　　　香港新界大埔汀麗路36號中華商務印刷大廈3字樓

印　　刷：中華商務彩色印刷有限公司
　　　　　香港新界大埔汀麗路36號中華商務印刷大廈14字樓

版　　次：2016年9月第1版第1次印刷
　　　　　© 2016 商務印書館（香港）有限公司
　　　　　ISBN 978 962 07 0471 0
　　　　　Printed in Hong Kong
　　　　　版權所有　不得翻印